Second Chance Beach

by

Pam Binder

Folly Beach

by

Darcy Carson

Vines to Water

by

DeeAnna Galbraith

**A Collection of Sweet and Sensual
Beach Romances**

written by
Pam Binder
Darcy Carson
DeeAnna Galbraith

Edited, arranged, and published by

Reads Publishing

Contact information:
Pam Binder, pambinder.com,
Darcy Carson, darcycarsonbooks.com, and
DeeAnna Galbraith, deeannagalbraith.com

Cover art by Angela Carson

Print ISBN: 978-1-7350188-0-5

Digital ISBN: 978-1-7350188-1-2

Second Chance Beach

By Pam Binder

Dedication

To my sister, Marilyn.
We fought as children,
gave each other a second chance,
and now we are best friends.

Chapter One

A Recipe for a successful match:

Begin with a mixture of friendship,

Communication and respect.

Add a generous dash of attraction.

Blend equal parts of commitment,

Trust and honesty,

And fold in a heaping cup of love.

"Love is easy," Cassy said aloud to her cat. "Finding, accepting, and holding onto love is the hard part."

Her cat, Charmer, purred in agreement as Cassy settled at her kitchen table. Charmer looked like the owls from the Harry Potter series with his long silver fur, lop ears, and in many ways, just as wise. Cassy reached for her reading glasses as she looked out the window at the setting sun reflecting over the water. She loved the view of the Kirkland marina and the boats docked on Lake Washington.

Cassy smiled and pushed her rhinestone glasses up the bridge of her nose as she gathered the photos on the table and waited for her sisters, Isadora, and Shawna. They had a big evening ahead of them. Tonight was the wedding reception for one of their success stories, and Cassy had just received word their new client was attending the party.

Her mother had been right to encourage Cassy and her two sisters to expand their cousin's matchmaking business in this area. Their cousins, Roselyn, Bridget, and Fiona focused on new love, while Cassey and her sisters concentrated on those seeking a second chance.

Like her cousins, Cassy and her sisters had been matchmakers all their lives and had the magic touch when it came to connecting people with their soulmates. If they ran into trouble, their cat, Charmer, was there to help.

Her two sisters entered the kitchen, Isadora carrying a tray of sweet rolls, Shawna, a basket of gemstone bracelets she had made as party favors for the reception tonight.

Shawna set the basket on the table. "What's the progress on Eric and Elizabeth? Have they made first contact yet?"

Cassy frowned as she selected a chocolate-covered donut from Isadora, set it on her plate and licked her fingers. "Listen to you. You sound like NASA. No, our couple has not made 'first contact.' If all goes well, that will happen tonight at the wedding reception for Elizabeth's father and his new bride."

Isadora took a bite of her cream-filled donut and sighed. "This is so good. Is it true Elizabeth and Eric knew each other in high school?"

Cassy poured tea into her cup and nodded. "We learned about them from a happy accident when we were planning Elizabeth's father's wedding reception. He recognized Eric when he was docking his boat in the marina near our restaurant. It seems Elizabeth tutored Eric in high school, although they never dated."

Shawna tried on one of the green stone bracelets she had made and held it out to the light streaming from the window. "I still remember Eric's reaction when we showed him Elizabeth's picture. To Elizabeth, Eric was just another boy in her class who needed help with homework, but to Eric O'Shay, Elizabeth was the girl who got away."

Isadora looked over the donuts on the tray as though preparing to select another one. "That's is so romantic."

Cassy nodded. "Indeed. But there is no guarantee that Elizabeth will be attracted to Eric or that when he sees her, he will still feel the same. A lot of time has passed since they were in high school. They're not the same people. Now, what's the progress on our other couples?"

Chapter Two

Rain poured from the June night sky trying to break last month's record, as Elizabeth Sanders Powell turned into a parking lot near the Kirkland marina and turned off the ignition. The world was out of balance. That was the only explanation she could think of to describe her day as vice principal. She had managed to prevent a hysterical teacher from quitting because a student had brought a boa constrictor for show and tell, organize a fund raiser for the parents' club, and entertain students until their tardy parents picked them up after school. She was now an hour and a half late for her father's wedding reception and he would be furious.

She changed from her sensible black work pumps into the red stiletto heels she had bought for the occasion. She had also purchased a dress, but there had been no time to change from her dark work suit. At least her father would understand sensible work clothes.

Opening the car door and her umbrella in the same instant, she made a dash for the buildings across the street, only to have to wait on the sidewalk at the four way stop until the cars noticed her. She knew she would have a long wait. At this time of day people were in a hurry to get home.

She glanced at the time on her phone as she fished the invitation out of her purse looking for the address. Her father had remarried a few months ago in a quiet ceremony, and this party was a way to include their friends in their celebration. Cassy had been to the restaurant only once before but that had been in broad daylight and she had bumped into it by accident. It was located down a narrow alley that led to the beach and was visible only from the water side. It was not an easy place to find unless, of course, you owned a boat or knew someone who did.

She had known someone once with a boat: her ex fiancé. He had not left her at the altar, but close. Everyone in his group had boats and shared visions of marrying super models and traveling the world. She should not have been surprised when he-whose-name-she-would-never-say-again, dumped her for an NFL cheerleader. She was surprised, however, that it still hurt.

Cars sped past her, splashing water onto the sidewalk and Elizabeth's opened-toed stiletto heels. She grimaced, knowing her cute shoes were ruined. She hopped from one foot to the other to keep her feet warm. She'd been uncharacteristically distracted all day and guessed it must be her apprehension regarding her father's reception.

At least a portion of her apprehension had to do with the actual location of the party. It was an old warehouse that had been converted to its present incarnation, the Second Chance restaurant. During the weekdays, they served everything from fish and chips to Lobster Thermador, but they were famous for their garlic fries and fish tacos. Located in Kirkland, the restaurant overlooked Lake Washington and was a ten-mile drive from Seattle, a city that bragged coffee shops multiplied faster in the Puget Sound area than rabbits.

Everyone knew the three sisters who owned the establishment did more than serve fish and cater parties. They were the newest import from Ireland and their primary job was as the city's matchmakers. Maybe that was the real reason she was late. The last time she had been there they had bombarded her with questions on the past men in her life. The conversation hadn't taken long but it had made Elizabeth uncomfortable. She didn't like dredging up the past. There were too many painful memories.

She held onto her umbrella as though it were a lifeline. Seeking advice from a matchmaker was fine for some, but Elizabeth was not interested, and she had told them so in no uncertain terms. When she had graduated from college, her father had cautioned her regarding relationships, claiming they tended to come between a person and their ambitions. He brought up her ex as the perfect example. At age twenty-eight, she still agreed with her father. Even though his recent heart attack had changed his philosophy on the subject drastically, Elizabeth still felt his caution regarding relationships held merit. She was living proof.

Elizabeth was the proud owner of a two-bedroom condominium and a kind cat named Princess she had rescued from an animal shelter. She had done well on her principal internship this last year and had her choice of job offers. Elizabeth was well on her way to? achieving her goals of becoming a principal and one day a superintendent of schools. Life was good.

Traffic lightened and she seized the opportunity and ran across the street. Reaching the sidewalk, she paused to reread the address on the invitation, but it was too dark. Nothing looked familiar. Did she have the wrong street? She knew the restaurant faced the marina, but that encompassed most of the shoreline.

In the dark everything looked the same. A street lamp was burned out and the sidewalk was shrouded in shadows. She bent to dig for her phone in her purse and use the flashlight feature and heard a man's voice talking to someone on his phone.

The man was jogging in her direction.

Tall, broad shouldered with the fluid movements of a trained athlete, he raced straight for her as though she were invisible. His attention was on his phone and his head turned in the direction of the lake.

She spun on her heels as though she were still in ballet class. She managed to keep upright, but when she took a step back, her foot landed in a puddle. Murky water splashed on her legs as a gust of wind blew her umbrella inside out.

Perfect.

The man, still talking on his phone, sped away from her in the direction of Lake Washington. He had not so much as broken his stride. The incident conjured the times in high school when the baseball and football teams had jogged past her like she was roadkill. A few of the ones she had tutored were nice, and one stood out, but most of them were jerks.

A door opened, spilling light onto the sidewalk and a woman Elizabeth recognized as one of the owners smiled at her. It was Cassy. She did not fit the image Elizabeth had of matchmakers. In fact, none of the sisters did. They looked as though they were in their late forties or early fifties, with a faint Irish lilt to their voices. Cassy's white-blonde hair was chin-length and she wore a pink-sheath dress and matching jacket.

From Cassy's expression it was apparent she had not witnessed the near collision with the jogger and that was fine with Elizabeth. All she needed was for her father's friends to think his daughter was late, and a klutz.

Chapter Three

Eric O'Shay jogged past the music and hum of conversation and laughter at Party Central, as he liked to call the Second Chance restaurant. The sisters who ran the restaurant were always throwing events to celebrate love. They had even tried to rope him in on their matchmaking schemes, showing him pictures of potential soulmates. One picture had stood out.

He had recognized the woman at once. She had kind brown eyes, a brilliant smile that could brighten even the gloomiest day, and long dark hair that made a man want to run his fingers through the waves. But he had told them that he was not interested. He had tried love and it had let him down.

Rain poured from the dark sky in an endless torrent that scoffed at the notion this was the first day of summer. He ducked under a low hanging branch without slowing his pace as he slipped a letter into the pocket of his running shorts.

Retrieving the mail was the only reason he had gone out in this blasted rainy weather in the first place. He had been expecting a letter from his attorney regarding the custody of his six-year-old son. Eric had called his lawyer a few minutes ago but the man already had left for the day.

It was June, but it felt more like February. Normally, the weather would not have bothered him. He had trained in blistering heat and finger-numbing cold. He had been a catcher with the professional baseball team, the Seattle Islanders, and damned good at his job – until a shoulder injury derailed his season but with hope, not his career.

Now, he played the waiting game.

He splashed through ankle deep puddles and cut through an expanse of spongy grass. A lamppost over-looking the lake sputtered for a few seconds and went dark. He did not need even that meager amount of light to see where he was going. He had spent the last three months anchored here, and this area along the lake was as familiar to him as hitting a homerun or catching a throw from the short stop to tag out the runner. Between living on his boat and traveling to the physical therapist's office trying to rehab a torn rotator cuff, three months had seemed closer to three years. No wonder the weather bothered him. Everything bothered him these days.

The only bright spot was when his son, Liam, visited. Eric had bought a small house for those occasions. It was close to Liam's school, so that his son could still be around his friends.

He slowed his run to a walk, fighting off a wave of foreboding. If he could not play baseball anymore, what would he do?

Eric reached the gate that led to the finger pier where his powerboat was moored and whistled for his dog, Rookie.

An eighty-pound Golden Retriever raced down the pier. Eric smiled, thankful again for the impulse he had to buy the dog two years ago at his nephew's school auction. He had bought Rookie so that his son, Liam, could have a dog to play with when he visited.

Eric watched the dog race toward him. The pier was slick, yet Rookie ran as though the dock were bare, dry, and well-lit. Pride swelled within him: man, or beast, Eric respected the will to excel.

With his dog at his side, Eric punched in the keycode on the gate and jogged over to his boat. Forty-two feet and custom made to his specifications. He could afford one larger. Hell, he could afford a fleet of boats, but then he would have needed a crew, and he preferred to explore the Puget Sound and islands around the Canadian San Juans alone. You had to have skill and nerve to operate a boat this size, but Eric liked the challenge of having no one to count on but himself. That was the reason he liked being a catcher. He was the team's last line of defense.

Eric rubbed his shoulder. He had injured it during spring training. The coach was angry his starting catcher had wasted his arm by throwing too hard during a practice game, then compounded the injury by helping his sister coach a little league practice for nine- and ten-year-old children.

Eric only knew one way to play and that was full out. Besides, his luck had always held. He had survived injuries before and come back stronger than ever. This time would be no different.

Minor detail, this time his shoulder had not responded to surgery and physical therapy as quickly as it had in the past. He tried not to worry, but the truth was that he did not know what he would do if he could not play baseball. Endorsements would dry up and he had no interest in acting or becoming a sports commentator, let alone traveling the country as an inspirational speaker. High school and college coaching offers were starting to come in, but he was not sure he was ready to sit on the sidelines instead of participating in the game.

If he were awarded full custody of his six-year-old son, the choice would be easy. He would gladly settle down in one place. His son was the most important person in his life. But there were no guarantees and his lawyer was not hopeful.

Clouds drifted over the night sky, blocking out the moon and stars. Eric shook the dark foreboding away again. It was not like him to be so negative. It must be all the inactivity.

He glanced down at his dog. "Are you in the mood to extend our run?"

With Rookie's bark, Eric took off at a fast jog along the shoreline.

Chapter Four

C assy extended her hand and a smile as she invited Elizabeth inside the restaurant. "Elizabeth, you're drenched. You look as though you were swimming in Lake Washington. Come on inside before you catch a summer cold. We don't bite." She laughed. "At least I don't."

Elizabeth closed her umbrella and followed Cassy. The restaurant had been transformed from the last time she'd seen it into something out of a romantic fantasy. Well-loved leather chairs were pulled close to a cheery fire and lampshades were fringed with crystal and amethyst beads. Wood chairs were draped with plush green velvet and hugged tables that were covered with violet and red votive candles. There was a four-piece band playing in the far corner of the room and the lively music combined with the conversation and laughter. The mood was warm and inviting and made Elizabeth feel foolish for her earlier apprehension.

The restaurant was crowded with guests who were dressed casually in vibrant spring colors. Elizabeth hadn't had time to change and felt underdressed in her dark suit. It didn't matter, her father would understand, after all; he was the one who'd taught her work came first.

Cassy waved to her sisters, who were weaving toward them. Their eyes sparkled with mischief. There was something welcoming about the women that Elizabeth found difficult to define. Growing up without a mother or a sister, Elizabeth felt drawn to their warmth and good humor. It was like walking into a kitchen after someone had baked an apple pie. Isadora was tall and slender with an ageless grace and style that drew everyone's attention. She wore a long skirt and blouse in shades of summer. Shawna wore cream-colored slacks and a matching turtleneck sweater. She was the most elegant of the three with straight caramel-colored hair and a quiet, almost shy demeanor.

Shawna carried a basket filled with bracelets made from chips of glass and semi-precious stones. "Hello, Elizabeth, we're so glad you're here, now the party is really complete." Shawna held the basket out toward Elizabeth. "Be sure to take one of the bracelets. Cassy made them especially for this occasion as party favors. Just touching the stones makes a person feel more confident."

Cassy winked. "And a bit sexier. We're all wearing them." Cassy held out her arm. There were at least six or seven of the bracelets dangling from her wrist. The stones sparked and twinkled in the candle and firelight. "It's great for the love life. I keep hoping to find my very own Prince Charming one day." She scrunched her nose. "I've kissed my share of frogs. One stands out."

Elizabeth could relate. She slipped her hands into her pockets as the room closed in on her. Wearing jewelry was not her style. This was exactly the type of confrontation she was dreading. But she could certainly agree with the sisters on the whole kissing frogs scenario. "I'm not looking for romance and I gave up on fairy tales the same year I stopped believing in Santa Claus."

There was a collective sigh from all three sisters. Shawna was the first to recover. She shook her head slowly and lowered her voice. "Ah, well, that is too bad, but please choose one just the same. Your father insisted that every person at the reception wear a bracelet. You wouldn't want to disappoint him, would you?"

Isadora nodded toward Elizabeth. "It's all in good fun. What do you have to lose?"

Trapped. Elizabeth felt outnumbered and guessed the only way she was going to get rid of the three sisters was to agree. She eased her hands out of her pockets and reached for the nearest bracelet. Purple and rose-colored stones winked back at her and reflected off a silver clasp. The stones were warm to the touch and the bracelet fit her wrist as though it had been made for her. They reminded her of the bracelet she'd given her mother for Mother's Day.

Elizabeth flashed on her last memory of her mother. It had been a rainy day like this one. Elizabeth had been eight and helping her mother dress for a job interview across town. Her father had insisted her mother wear pearls and gold earrings for the interview, but Elizabeth had wanted her mother to wear the bracelet she'd given her for Mother's Day. Her mother had chosen the bracelet and her parents fought over her mother's decision.

Cassy interrupted Elizabeth's thoughts with a nudge. "Your father's been checking the door every few minutes waiting for you to arrive. He guessed there was a school emergency."

Elizabeth brushed at her eyes and placed the broken umbrella in a red and gold oriental urn by the window, making a mental note to try and repair it this weekend. "I was late because a parent was late picking up her child. I stayed until she arrived."

"Your father thought it might be something like that. Well, you're here now so go give your dad a big hug. I think he's over by the dance floor. I'd better help Shawna in the kitchen. There are more people at the reception than we expected." She laughed. "Shawna claims we're running out of food and is frantically emptying our cupboards."

Cassy nodded goodbye and Elizabeth watched as she weaved through the crowd smiling at everyone she passed by. Elizabeth thought over what Cassy had said. She'd wanted Elizabeth to give her father a hug. That was another new phase her father was going through. Her mother used to like to give hugs, but her father would go out of his way to avoid them. His aversion became even more pronounced when Elizabeth's mother had died in a car crash the day of the job interview.

Elizabeth remembered other things about her mother as well. Her long auburn hair that shimmered with light and her eyes the color of dark chocolate. Her dad always said Elizabeth looked like her mother more and more each day. Maybe so, but their life philosophies were as different as dog people and cat people. Case in point. Her mother had insisted playtime was as important as work time.

Elizabeth pushed her wet hair off her forehead and took a slow, even breath. What was the matter with her tonight? She was spending way too much time reminiscing. The past and all it represented should stay where it belonged, in the past.

Elizabeth walked through the crush of people in the direction Cassy had indicated. Most of the guests were friends her father had met at the restaurant. It was still hard remembering how her father had looked in the hospital bed a few months ago. She shook away the dark memories and focused on the fact that he'd made a full recovery.

The changes had been gradual at first. He'd turned over a lot of his duties to his assistant at his construction company, started exercising and eating better, and the dark circles under his eyes were disappearing. One day, after one of her visits, she noticed something even more remarkable. He was smiling and there was lightness in his step that was hard to miss. It was also the day he had told her he was getting married to Cynthia Grant, a woman he'd dated in high school. She was also a widow and a volunteer at the hospital where he had recovered from his heart attack.

Elizabeth passed a bulletin board framed in hearts, devoted to photos and schedules of events held at the restaurant. According to her father, if you were interested in finding someone, you tacked your picture on the wall. Most people thought it was a fun idea. Elizabeth believed it sent a signal to the world that you were alone and desperate. She was neither. She had plenty of time to find a husband when she decided it was time to get married and settle down.

A space cleared in the café and she saw her father laughing and dancing with his new bride. They had married in a small ceremony a month ago and had planned this big reception for when they returned from their honeymoon in Hawaii. Elizabeth really was pleased for her father.

Her father turned and smiled toward her. He was standing next to Cynthia holding her hand. He whispered to his new wife and they both headed in Elizabeth's direction.

Elizabeth had liked Cynthia from the moment her father had introduced them. She was a retired schoolteacher with white hair cropped close to a heart shaped face. Cynthia was always in a good mood. She and Elizabeth's father beamed at each other like school kids in the blush of young love.

Cynthia reached Elizabeth first and embraced her. "Elizabeth, we're so pleased you're here." "I'll second that." Her father's eyes brimmed with tears as he grabbed her in a crushing bear hug.

Elizabeth pushed against him gently until he released his hold. She managed a smile, still getting used to her father's changed attitude. "Me too."

He stood back and cleared his throat. "They're not working you too hard at the school are they, Elizabeth my girl?"

"No, everything is just the way it should be."

Cynthia patted him on the arm. "Now, Tom, even if she were working too hard, at her age would you have listened to anyone, or for that matter, thought to slow down?"

He smiled and kissed her hand. "Not a chance." He grew serious. "Are you happy, Elizabeth?"

Elizabeth was taken off guard. She didn't know how to respond. Thankfully, she didn't have to, as her father was distracted by the music.

The band had started again and Tom pulled Cynthia gently toward the center of the room. "Let's dance. They're playing our song."

Cynthia giggled. "You've said that about every song the band has played tonight."

His response to Cynthia was lost in the music and laughter as Elizabeth watched her father whisk Cynthia away. A cheer rang out from the crowd as he dipped his new wife on the dance floor. Her father was laughing, really laughing. Elizabeth realized she hadn't seen him that happy in a very long time, but why had he asked her if she was happy? Happiness was highly overrated and had very little to do with a person's career or life goals.

Two of her father's golfing buddies appeared out of the crowd. That was another new phenomenon. Her father used to say golf was a waste of time, but after the heart attack he'd renewed college friendships and taken up the game.

The men shook Elizabeth's hand in turn and told her the same thing they had whenever they saw her. They told her she looked more and more like her mother every day, except that she was getting too thin. Their smiling wives joined the buzz of conversation and pictures of grandchildren were shoved toward her.

When the conversation turned toward questions of who Elizabeth was dating, she changed the subject and told them she needed to say hello to the other guests.

She made her escape only to have her path blocked by a cat. The silver fur ball brushed against her ankles. Elizabeth bent down, welcoming the distraction as the animal purred contentedly in her arms as she picked him up.

"Well, now," Elizabeth said, "you're a welcome surprise."

The cat rubbed his head against her hand. Elizabeth smiled. "You could teach my cat, Princess, a thing or two about being friendly. She behaves as though I should feel honored to serve her."

The cat closed his eyes and purred, leaning his head against her hand again as Cassy came up beside Elizabeth. "I see you've met Charmer. He's a bit of a scamp at times, but we don't know what we'd do without the lad." She motioned toward Cynthia and Elizabeth's father. "They make such a happy couple, don't you think?"

Elizabeth cradled Charmer in her arms and nodded. "Thank you for all you've done for my father."

Cassy smiled. "You're welcome, but your father and Cynthia were one of our easier matches."

"I thought they met at the hospital?"

Cassy nodded. "They did, but neither was ready to believe what they felt for each other was the real thing. Some people need a second chance. That's where my sisters and I come in."

Elizabeth was still not sure about the whole, matchmaker concept, but she couldn't deny the happiness she saw reflected in her father's eyes. Well, if it worked for him, who was she to criticize? But she knew something like this would not work for her. The moment the thought had left her, Shawna and Isadora joined Cassy and were hustling her to the Matchmaker Wall.

Cassy pointed to a jumbled collection of photos of men who ranged in age and appearance. "My hobby is taking pictures. It comes in handy in our business. Do you see anyone who looks interesting?"

The pictures all blurred together, and the men looked the same. Their smiles were too broad and their eyes too intense. Slowly, Elizabeth shook her head. She was struggling to be kind to the sisters because of how they'd helped her father.

Shawna plucked one of the pictures off the wall and shoved it under Elizabeth's nose. "He's cute. What about him?"

Isadora grabbed the photo away from Shawna and tacked it back on the board. "He's already taken. Besides, we can't do the choosing anymore, remember?"

Shawna folded her arms. "Stupid rule."

Isadora drew in a slow breath. "Regardless, this is a choice Elizabeth has to make. We can't choose for her."

Shawna sighed. "Our grandmother used to tell us in her day matchmaking was much simpler. We'd make the decision for the couples."

Cassy flipped her hair over her shoulder. "Well, I for one am glad times have changed. Can you imagine marrying a perfect stranger?" She shuddered. "How would you know if the two of you were compatible in bed?"

Shawna cleared her throat. "Well, I for one think it's more important if the person is responsible, trustworthy…"

Cassy interrupted. "Elizabeth is not thinking about buying a dog. She wants a man who is hot blooded, passionate, and sensitive to all her needs."

Isadora put her hand on Cassy's arm and turned toward Shawna. "Sisters, we are not talking about what you want but what interests Elizabeth."

Elizabeth backed away from the wall. "Actually, I'm not interested in anyone now. My life is full enough without adding any unnecessary baggage."

All three sisters spoke at once. "Baggage?"

"Interesting," Cassy murmured. "I've never thought of a man as 'baggage' before. Is that an American expression?"

Elizabeth turned, leaving the three sisters mumbling to themselves as she headed through the restaurant toward a back door, the lake, and freedom. This was exactly the reason she had been so reluctant to visit the restaurant in the first place. The sisters had the reputation of being relentless in their quest to find everyone a mate.

Elizabeth had no intention of being one of their statistics. Her life was full. No time in it for distractions. But somewhere in the back of her mind, glistening like the stones on her bracelet, was the thought there might be something missing. Her mother believed in a balance between work and play, but then her mother had never been the ambitious type. Her father was the one who understood her, the one who had guided her after her mother's death. True, his heart attack had changed him, but not until he'd achieved all his goals.

Elizabeth walked along the path leading toward the lake. A thick coating of stars dusted the night sky and reflected over Lake Washington, illuminating the large sailboats and powerboats moored at the dock. Elizabeth stood outside the restaurant and took a deep breath; the storm had passed, and the air smelled fresh and clean.

She slipped off her high heels and dangled the straps on her fingers as she walked aimlessly along the boardwalk. The cool wet surface felt good on her bare feet. The music and laughter coming from the direction of the reception filled the night air, blending in with the occasion muffled conversation. A cool breeze blew off the water, rippling its calm surface. She should feel relieved to be away from the crush of people attending her father's party. Instead, she was restless.

A dog's bark broke through the still night air. Elizabeth turned toward the sound. On a boat a few yards away, a Golden Retriever peered over the railing of one of the largest powerboats Elizabeth had ever seen. A man stood beside the dog, patting the animal on the head. When he pulled the dog away from the railing, Elizabeth's heart skipped a beat. The man's face was lost in the shadows, but he wasn't wearing a shirt and in the moonlight his muscles looked as though they were chiseled out of stone. His hair was dark and unkempt and his smile infectious as he played with his dog. She wondered how his arms would feel around her body. Would his kisses awaken her passion? Was he a good lover?

"Whoa," she said aloud. "Where did that come from?"

She blamed the matchmakers and her father's marriage. She had not thought about dating, or the fantasy of a happily-ever-after, in a very long time.

She veered away from the boat and headed toward one of the finger piers. Her head ached with tumbling thoughts. She tried to push them away, but it was no use. One thought stood out amongst all the others. Her father had asked her if she was happy. She had not known how to respond.

She was glad he had not asked her if she was lonely. She knew the answer to that question.

Chapter Five

The longer jog along the shoreline had worked its magic. Eric had not solved all his problems but at least he felt calmer. He stepped onto the deck of his boat and whistled for Rookie.

The dog bounded from the water and raced toward the boat, leaping onto the deck.

"For once, I beat you on board, old friend."

Rookie barked as though to warn Eric there would be no second time.

Eric laughed for what seemed the first time in months. It felt good. He stood his ground and tousled the dog's head. Four years old and Rookie still acted like a puppy. The dog had a long list of bad habits Eric's brother and sister were quick to point out. Rookie slept on Eric's bed, never on his own, and ate his older brother's shoes.

The worst, Eric admitted, was the barking. Eric still had not managed to break Rookie from the habit of barking at anything that moved or breathed. Eric knew he was partially responsible, as he had not tried that hard to break the barking habit. Maybe it was because Eric could see his dog's point. Sometimes you had to be free to speak your mind.

Eric rubbed his injured shoulder. That philosophy had gotten him into trouble in his career as well as his failed marriage. He was trying to change, and he knew it was a cliché to say that he had felt the change begin when his son was born, but it was the truth. The moment his little man wrapped his hand around Eric's finger, Eric's world and his priorities shifted.

Rookie shook his body, spraying water in every direction. Eric laughed, taking off his shirt. "Thanks for the shower, pal. Is that payback for the crack about my beating you to the boat? Fair enough. Are you hungry? I know I am."

Rookie barked in response. Eric paused to scratch the dog behind his ear before walking over and opening the cabin door. He did not believe in locks. His outlook did not have so much to do with trusting people as the reality that he was always forgetting where he had left his keys.

The moment the door was open, Rookie trotted past Eric through the cabin and straight for the galley and his dog dish.

Eric smiled. "Hold on, I'm coming."

He ducked his head. The opening was not tall enough to accommodate his height, but it was a minor inconvenience he lived with. Owning a boat was better than the alternative of living in a house or a condo-minium. He had always disliked the idea of being confined to one place. He liked the idea that he could weigh anchor and take his home with him wherever and whenever the impulse struck him. The whole idea of setting down roots used to give him the cold shivers. If he were granted full custody of his son, though, he would gladly settle down.

Rookie barked. This time, the bark seemed important.

Eric glanced toward his dog and paused, thumbing through his mail. "Give me a minute, pal." Eric held a letter in one hand and tossed the rest onto a chair. The letter was from his attorney. He stared at the attorney's formal envelope, with its embossed logo, until his vision blurred.

He wanted to rip it open, like a Band-Aid from a wound. He held back. His ex-wife had agreed Eric could have full custody of their son. Her modeling career had taken off and her new boyfriend/agent thought her son was a distraction. But she could have changed her mind.

Their son was six and they had been divorced for four years. They had shared joint custody, but he had lost track of the times when she had called to ask Eric to pick their son up at a photoshoot, or to take care of him because she was going out of town. He never minded. The more time he could spend with his son the better.

Rookie nudged Eric's hand and wagged his tail.

Eric shook his head. "I'll read it later." He opened the kitchen drawer and threw it on top of mail and a ring-size package he'd received from his grandmother a few weeks ago. His grandmother had included a note that instructed him to give it to the woman he loved. A tall order. He had to find her first.

"Okay, pal," Eric said, "you have my full attention. I will open the letter later, maybe after I've had a beer. What will it be tonight? Dry kibble for you and frozen dinner for me?" Rookie barked again and wagged his tail as though Eric had announced they were both having steak. Eric laughed. "That's what I like about you, pal: you're easy to please."

Without warning, Rookie rushed past Eric and headed for the door. Eric stepped aside. "Hey, where're you going?"

Once outside, Rookie's bark changed in tempo and depth. The dog was in full watchdog mode, giving the impression that Eric's boat was about to be boarded by a band of pirates or in danger of bursting into flames. Eric followed close behind and glanced around. The rain had stopped, but the storm had succeeded in discouraging people from strolling along the pier. The waterfront was deserted except for a woman walking aimlessly along the dock barefoot. The sway of her hips and the way her long, dark hair swept over her shoulders were familiar somehow. He edged to the railing to try and get a closer look as she disappeared behind one of the boats.

Rookie barked again.

Eric pulled the dog down from the side of the boat "What's got into you tonight? You're barking more than normal." Rookie strained against Eric's grip, but he held the dog in place. "Hey, pal, I appreciate the whole watchdog attitude, but you're barking at some lady walking barefoot. I guarantee we're not in any danger, but if you keep this up, you're likely to get us evicted."

He rubbed the back of his neck. There were rules attached to being allowed to moor a boat this size at the Kirkland marina and most of them referred to pets. Because of Eric's status as a professional baseball player, exceptions had been made, special privileges extended. But even that good will, Eric was smart enough to figure out, had its limits. He needed to stay where he was until his shoulder was rehabbed and then he'd leave this rain-soaked city for good. Playing for a Florida teamed appealed to him and he could fly his siblings and mom out to the sunshine whenever they wanted to visit. He paused to pat Rookie on the head and made his decision. He would call his agent in the morning.

Rookie broke free of Eric's grasp and put his front paws on the side of the boat again. The dog was barking in short deep bursts. In the distance Eric heard a cat screech. Naturally, Rookie barked in response.

Eric ground out his words. "This has to stop." He pulled the dog down and led him into the cabin. "Great. Now you're barking at a defenseless cat. First thing tomorrow morning I'm enrolling you in obedience school."

Eric looked over his shoulder and paused. Despite the storm earlier, the air was still, as though it was holding its breath. He swore to himself. He did not blame Rookie for being so hyper. No doubt the dog could sense that his owner was losing his grip on reality.

Chapter Six

A silver-gray cat meowed and darted past Elizabeth along the finger pier. Startled, Elizabeth rolled back on her heels, then regained her balance. She recognized the animal. It was Cassy's cat, Charmer. He scampered in front of Elizabeth then angled toward the lake.

The pier was slippery from the rain earlier that night, and the cat was skidding over the slick boards toward the water's edge. His plight reminded Elizabeth of how her cat, Princess, had looked when she had tried to run on a freshly polished wood floor, regaining her balance only moments before she would have crashed into a wall. Elizabeth hoped Charmer would have the same good fortune.

Charmer's meow changed in tone and tempo until his cry for help rose over the music and laughter of the reception. In the next instant, Charmer was airborne and landed in the water with a loud splash.

Elizabeth rushed to the edge of the dock. A circle of ripples spread out from where the cat had landed near the pier. She called his name and the seconds ticked by until she spotted him surfacing a short distance away. She sighed with relief just as a new fear set in. She did not think cats liked to swim. He thrashed around in the water with a wild expression in his eyes.

She looked around. Just her luck, the dock was deserted. The man on the boat had disappeared into that floating condominium and obviously had not heard the commotion his dog had caused. She glanced once more toward Charmer. Years of swim lessons had resulted in her ability to float on her back if the water was calm. She groaned, knowing she could not let him drown.

Easing down on the dock Elizabeth tried to reach the cat by extending her arm, but Charmer's efforts to keep his head above the water only succeeded in moving him farther away. If Elizabeth hadn't known better, she would have sworn Charmer was trying to coax her into the water. Ridiculous.

Elizabeth inched her way forward until her body teetered lengthwise along the pier and stretched out toward him. She struggled to keep her precarious balance, sensing she was hanging too far over the edge. It could not be helped. She would not let Charmer drown. She stretched out farther and then it happened.

Elizabeth let out a scream, tumbling into the icy water.

She plunged downward, surprised how freezing the lake was for June. Instinctively, she kicked back to the surface and gasped for breath. This was just great.

No doubt she'd wake up Monday morning with a cold. In addition, her legs kept tangling in the thick underwater plants, making it difficult to tread water. She used her arms to keep her head above the surface and looked around, expecting to see the cat nearby.

She reached a new level of frustration.

The little beast had managed to swim toward the dock and was in the process of climbing to safety. Charmer shook off the water, turned toward her and paused before padding off in the direction of the café as though nothing had happened.

Elizabeth swore under her breath. She took back every good thing she'd said about the cat. She kicked but her legs were still tangled, as though the plants were trying to drag her under.

She splashed in the water in much the same way as the cat had moments before and with the same result. She did not know how much longer she could keep her head above the water.

She gulped in water, choked, then screamed.

"Help. Somebody. Anybody!"

Chapter Seven

A t this time of night, the public dock was deserted. Elizabeth's cries for help were drowned out by the sounds of seagulls and the music and laughter coming from her father's reception. Hoping a couple was taking a romantic stroll along the pier; Elizabeth took in another deep breath and screamed again. Her voice echoed through the still night air and held on the breeze.

Elizabeth gasped for breath as she went under for the second time, swallowing a mouthful of icy water. Her legs were tangled in dense weeds and the harder she tried to free herself the tighter their grip grew. Trying to kick free, she fought a growing panic.

Who would feed her cat if she drowned? Who would the principal assign to finish the teacher evaluations? And why did she think it was so strange that after all this time her dad liked to give hugs?

She screamed again.

A seagull answered her cry with a frightful caw. He seemed to be scolding her for her foolishness in trying to save the matchmaker sister's cat from drowning.

Elizabeth fought back tears. Her shoulders ached and she was losing sensation in her arms. Never a good swimmer, she knew she was tiring rapidly, and floating was not an option. She was anchored in place by the dense rope-like plants growing on the surface of the lake. Elizabeth was like the boats tied along the finger piers, bobbing, and rocking with the currents. The only difference being she was losing the battle to stay afloat.

It was Friday evening, and no one would miss her until she failed to show up for work on Monday. Even her father had learned she preferred to spend her weekends catching up on paperwork and errands. She had never felt so alone.

The seagull cawed again, but this time she agreed with the bird. She was behaving like some helpless creature. It was not like her to give up so easily. "Stop it," she yelled and was pleased when he flapped his wings and flew away.

She took a deep breath and with renewed determination, kicked with all her strength. She ground her teeth, fighting through the burning in her muscles until she broke free. She let a sigh of relief. In a combination of dog paddle and crawl stroke she inched toward the pier. Next weekend she would sign up for swim lessons or make a solemn vow never to go near the water again.

She heard a splash nearby and out of the corner of her eye saw a man dive into the lake. Someone had come to her rescue after all. It was reassuring to know there were still hero-types left in the world. But this time she had not needed one: she had saved herself. Elizabeth smiled with self-satisfaction that she was not the damsel in distress type.

Her hand grazed the wood ladder attached to the dock. It was slick to the touch. She shuddered and gripped it tighter. She did not want to embarrass herself in front of her would-be rescuer by falling back into the lake after her valiant effort. Elizabeth gritted her teeth again and climbed onto the dock. She sat exhausted, shivering from the cold, and catching her breath, just as the man surfaced a short distance away and swam toward her.

Her heart did that flip-quiver-flip thing that she had not felt since college. He was the man she had been lusting over a few moments ago. Not good. She always made a fool of herself around handsome men. She wondered if she had time to make an escape before he reached the dock.

Almost before she had finished her thought, Mr. Knight in Running Shorts reached the pier, ignored the ladder, and bolted up on the dock in one fluid motion. He was dripping wet, bare chested, and his running shorts were soaked against muscular legs and riding low on his hips. She would bet the chocolate donut she had for breakfast this morning that he was naked underneath those clinging running shorts.

She swallowed, feeling her face flame.

He shook his wet hair out of his eyes and grinned. "I guess you didn't need my help," he said in a deep voice that vibrated down to her toes.

Her teeth chattered so hard she could only shake her head.

His voice quieted with concern as he knelt beside her. "Are you all right?"

She nodded.

His voice and manner put her at ease. What was more, he had jumped into the water to rescue her, and it looked as though he wasn't leaving until he knew she was all right. She had always considered herself independent and self-assured, but she had to admit having a handsome, attentive guy playing the role of a white knight was growing on her.

He brushed the hair off her forehead. "Can you stand?"

"I think...so."

He wrapped his arm around her waist and helped her to her feet. The man was well over six foot three with a bare chest and wearing a pair of clinging running shorts. Elizabeth's legs felt wobbly and unsteady. She tried to tell herself it was from her scare but knew it was more than that. She was five feet ten inches in her bare feet, and this tall, almost naked man was making her knees go school-girl-crush weak. She brushed her wet hair off her face, knowing her suit was ruined and whatever makeup she'd applied was washed off by her unscheduled swim.

He was dripping wet too, but on him it looked good. Nice It was a conspiracy and Mother Nature was in on it. Elizabeth shivered, half with cold and half with excitement.

"You're freezing." Rubbing her arms and hands he smiled. "What were you doing in the water anyway?"

Her teeth chattered again. "I was trying to save… a…a…cat."

He glanced around the dock and paused and then swore under his breath. "I'll bet my dog's responsible. He was barking and probably frightened it." He paused. "Where is the cat?"

Elizabeth shook her head and shivered again as a breeze blew against her wet skin. "The cat's fine." She managed a smile. "He didn't need my help. He rescued himself."

He laughed and the corners of his eyes crinkled. "There seems to be a lot of that going around." He grinned and reached down, picking up her shoes and holding them toward her. "Yours?"

"Oh, yes." She frowned. Her one indulgence in the world of high fashion was ruined. She should have followed logic and worn her more sensible shoes to the party.

His eyebrows knitted together. "They're sexy, but how can you walk in these things?"

She decided she'd made the right selection tonight after all. "Not very well I'm afraid. I was attending the wedding reception for my father and his new wife at the Second Chance restaurant and thought I should wear heels. I'm more of a sandals and tennis shoe kind of girl."

"Awesome." He laughed again and she loved the way it made her feel. It was friendly and open and familiar as though she had heard that laugh before. She dismissed the idea. She would not have forgotten someone this good looking.

"My name's Eric..." He hesitated and instead of supplying his last name, he held out his hand.

Placing her hand in his, she risked a smiled. "I'm Elizabeth Sanders Powell."

Time slowed and the sound of the waves lapping against the pilings amplified in her ears. His hand felt warm and solid and exciting as his fingers wrapped around hers. Her legs buckled again.

"I've got you." Eric put his arm around her waist and hesitated. "Is there a husband or fiancé waiting for you at the party?"

Elizabeth shook her head and her legs threatened to give way altogether. When his smile broadened, she knew she was officially in trouble.

"May I call you Beth?"

She hesitated, staring into his gray-green eyes. "I'm used to Elizabeth." She had learned her parents had spent a long time debating over what to call their daughter. Finally, at her mother's insistence, Elizabeth was named after her maternal grandmother, Elizabeth Sanders. It was a family name full of expectation and comparisons that she had learned to grow into. In school she had hoped one of her friends would shorten it, or at the very least, give her a nickname. No one ever had.

He leaned forward, so close she thought he'd read her mind. "Maybe you'll let me call you Beth when we get to know each other better."

She let out her breath slowly, not willing to let him in so quickly. "Yes, when we get to know each other better."

Eric straightened and nodded toward the large powerboat. "That's mine. I'm told I make a good cup of coffee. Can I offer you a cup? It's the least I can do after the trouble my dog caused. Besides, you look like you're freezing. Or would you rather return to the party?"

Seconds sped by as laughter from the wedding reception drifted over on the cool breeze. Elizabeth glanced in the direction of the sound. She was outside, she was drenched to the bone, but somehow, she felt warmer in Eric's presence than she had in the crowded reception room. She should say no to his offer and whatever else was behind that gleam in his eyes.

He had tried to save her, she reasoned, and returning to the restaurant was not an option. She was dripping wet and would have to admit to her klutzy behavior and be enveloped in well-meaning sympathy. It was not the best image for a soon-to-be principal, and going home to an empty condo held even less appeal. Besides, it was only coffee.

Satisfied that she was being logical, she made her decision, feeling bold. "Coffee sounds wonderful."

His smile creased the corners of his eyes. "Coffee it is, then."

Chapter Eight

Elizabeth felt acutely aware of Eric's presence as they strolled in the direction of his boat. His smile was making her shiver and the way she felt had nothing to do with her plunge into Lake Washington and everything to do with the way he kept looking at her.

Eric nodded in the direction of the restaurant. "How was the party?"

"It was my father's wedding reception. My mom died a long time ago and he just remarried."

He raised his eyebrow. "Was that weird? I mean your dad remarrying?"

She twisted the stone bracelet on her wrist. She had just met Eric and he'd asked her a personal question not many of her friends would have dared. "Are you always this blunt?"

"I'm sorry. It's a bad habit." He looked so contrite it made her smile.

She put her hand on his arm. "No, that's all right, really. Your question just caught me off guard. The truth is that I'm really fine with my father remarrying and his new wife, Cynthia, is wonderful. She makes him happy. It's just that…" She paused. "He's changed, and I need time to adjust."

"Good change or bad change?"

She strolled beside him for a few seconds exploring his question. How did she feel? Her father had hugged her, and she had been so startled that she had been the first to pull away in shock. When her mother died her father had withdrawn as though to protect himself from more pain. If she were being honest, she'd done exactly the same thing.

"I like the change," she admitted.

He nodded. "That's cool. And you were great to accept my apology, but my question really was too personal and none of my business."

"Actually, it feels good to talk about it. And you did try to save me from drowning."

He laughed softly. "I did, didn't I?"

She mirrored his smile and took in a deep breath. "All my friends dance around the issue as though I'll self-destruct. I think it's because you are a complete stranger that I feel comfortable talking about this with you. Here goes. My mother died in a car crash when I was eight and it's taken my father a long time to find happiness."

Eric paused beside his powerboat. "Let me guess. The matchmakers introduced your father to the love of his life."

"Something like that. How'd you know?"

He leaned toward her until their shoulders brushed. "Ever since those three sisters breezed into town their restaurant has been busy with weddings and wedding receptions. People walk in single and leave engaged. I'm not sure what's in the coffee they serve, but I started making my own, just in case. They're always coming by and showing me photos. They asked if they could pin a picture of me on their bulletin board."

Elizabeth shook her head. "They wanted my picture to pin on their bulletin board as well. I declined, but my father handed them an old photo he carried in his wallet."

"I can understand why the sisters wanted your photo. You're beautiful. You'd have every guy within a hundred-mile radius calling you for a date."

The compliment caught her off guard. Even on her best days, with full makeup and her hair profess-ionally curled, the most she had heard from men, including her ex fiancé, was that they liked her outfit. She knew she was plain and the type of person who faded into the scenery, especially if there were cheer-leaders in the foreground.

She pressed her hand against her stomach. It was quivering as though she had swallowed butterflies. She was dripping wet. Her wet hair was plastered against her face, and her clothes clung to her in unflattering bunches.

And yet he was flirting with her as though she was a model dressed for a New York fashion runway.

It was exhilarating and confusing at the same time. She should be polite and tell him she was too busy for coffee. She should tell him she had changed her mind. After all, she had to get back to... She struggled to think of a reason. "I should be going home to Princess."

"Princess?"

"My cat... And I have paperwork."

He paused and leaned forward until she could feel his warm breath on her skin. "It's Friday night, Elizabeth. What kind of boss makes you do paperwork on a Friday? Give me his name and I'll have him reported to the Date Police. If there isn't a law about a beautiful woman staying home on a Friday night, there should be."

Eric nudged her on the shoulder gently. "Live a little. Take the night off."

He'd smiled again and it most definitely lit up his eyes. Not good. She was thinking the combination gray-green was her new favorite color. It was confirmed. She had gone over the edge and was in a state of extreme infatuation.

Eric motioned to the boat behind him. "Well, here we are. This is where I live. She's called *Slugger*."

Without thinking she laughed out loud. "*Slugger?* You have got to be kidding. I thought boats had names like *Seaward* or *Lady of the Lake*."

He shrugged and smiled good naturedly. "What can I say? I'm a professional baseball player. I bought this boat a short time after my son turned two and my teammates commented that I would call him either my little man or slugger because he loved to practice baseball with me. I'd toss him a ball and he'd take his bat and make contact. I was always bragging, still do, by the way, that he was a natural born ball player. Slugger seemed the perfect name for my boat."

"You named your boat after your son." She loved that he was a father but felt as though someone had thrown a bucket of ice water over her head. "You're married."

"Divorced."

She let out her breath. "How old is your son now?"

"He turns four and told me this week that he no longer plans to be a professional baseball player. His new goal is firefighter. Naturally, I went out and bought him complete firefighter uniform in his size."

She grinned back at him. "Naturally."

Elizabeth really hadn't thought about what kind of occupation Eric had, but she could honestly say that a professional athlete was not on her preferred list of jobs for possible mates. Her ex had dreams of playing football after college, but college football was as far as he got. Eric had a son and from the way his eyes softened with a smile when he talked about him, Eric's son was important to him, and that set Eric apart in her mind.

A dog barked and she glanced in the direction of his boat. A large Golden Retriever had his front paws perched on the side of Eric's boat.

"Is that your dog?"

He nodded. "Yes, I'm afraid so. I'm sure Rookie barked at the cat. He likes to bark. It's his thing." Rookie barked as though acknowledging he knew Eric was talking about him. Eric laughed and yelled at Rookie to be quiet, then turned toward Elizabeth. "Do you like dogs?"

"I'm not sure." She had always heard dogs were messy and a lot of trouble. It was the reason she had a cat.

"From your expression I take it you don't like sports or dogs."

Elizabeth smiled at the serious expression on his face. "I never said I didn't like sports."

"You didn't have to."

Elizabeth should refuse his invitation. This would never work. He might be good looking, gallant, and easy to talk to, and a dad, but they had nothing in common. For starters, he was a dog person and she was a cat person.

When Eric jumped onto his boat, then held out his arms, she reached toward him, placing her hands on his shoulders. He lifted her onto the deck as though she were as light as starlight. Nice His eyes did that smolder thing she had only read about in romance novels or in chic movies. Her pulse raced.

Eric brushed her hair off her forehead as his voice deepened. "I have to tell you that independent women are a real turn on. I'm glad I tried to rescue you."

He kept saying all the right things. She cleared her throat. "Me too."

Her lips parted. She had never kissed a man first before. The thought quickened the already erratic beat of her heart. Should she, or shouldn't she? Eric pulled her closer against his bare chest. His heartbeat raced against her own. Her tongue moistened her lower lip as she rose on her tiptoes. Waves lapped against the side of his boat, rocking it gently.

She leaned into him.

Time slowed.

Rookie let out two short rounds of barks.

Eric drew back, raked his fingers through his hair, and sighed. "Great timing, pal."

Elizabeth straightened her soggy suit, smiling nervously. She was finding it difficult to breathe. "Maybe we should have that coffee now." Things were moving too fast. She wanted to slow down, if only to catch her breath.

He nodded and rubbed his eyes as though to clear them. "That perfume you're wearing fogs the brain."

"I'm not wearing any perfume."

He sucked in his breath. "I was afraid of that."

Eric reached for her hand and helped her step onto the deck, then drew her into the main cabin of the boat. He crossed the compact living quarters toward the galley. Other than a built-in desk toward her right, the cabin was devoid of furniture. So much for her bachelor lair theory. She was pleased and then reminded herself that it should not matter one way or the other.

"You don't have any furniture," she said.

Eric plugged in the electric coffeemaker and rummaged around in one of the cupboards, grabbing a canister. "Rookie considers sofas and chairs his own personal chew toys. I got tired of replacing them. Besides, I don't have that many visitors." He paused. "When my son comes, we stay at my house in the city near his school."

The silence hung in the air between them. The fact that he had mentioned his son again told her how important he was to Eric. "You bought a house near your son's school? That is amazing. How often do you get to see him?"

A shadow crossed over his features. "Not often enough. I'm hoping that will change. I received a letter from my attorney regarding my being granted full custody. I just haven't opened it."

She would not press him on the letter. She could see how worried he was about the contents. Rookie bounded beside her and wagged his tail. He nuzzled against her hand. She responded automatically and scratched him behind his ear. "Although Princess is a sweetheart, and great company, she always looks as though she's been startled by fairies. Your dog looks like he's smiling."

"It's Rookie's secret weapon. He knows I can't stay mad." He held her gaze as though wrestling with a question he wanted to ask. "You're being here feels like a good omen. The letter is in the top kitchen drawer. Would you mind opening it for me?"

She nodded slowly before heading to the drawer he had indicated. She opened the drawer that was a catch-all of car keys, pens, pads of papers, and odds and ends, including what looked like a flyer for a high school reunion at Bellevue High School. She pulled out the letter with an attorney's logo. She hesitated, feeling the weight in the room. She stared at the envelope and changed the subject. "You went to Bellevue. So did I."

"Is that right?" he said as she handed him the letter. "Now or never." He tore it opened. The seconds ticked by as she watched the play of emotions over his face. When he looked over at her she knew the answer even before he said the words.

He picked her up in his arms and spun her around the room. He set her down on the floor, his face beaming. "I was granted full custody. No strings."

Her heart swelled with joy for his good news. "Eric, I'm so happy for you. That is wonderful news."

"How do you like your coffee?"

"Strong."

"You're wish, milady, is my command."

There was something about Eric that made her heart beat faster. It wasn't only that he looked capable of sailing his boat around the globe in a hurricane. There was electricity in the air around him that made her feel more alive in his presence than she had with anyone else she'd ever known. She knew she was in dangerous territory but did not want to turn back now when it was just getting interesting. And if she was being honest, it wasn't his good looks that had her heart hammering: it was the look of love in his eyes when he talked about his son.

"Are you hungry?" he said.

Elizabeth was startled out of her daze. "Pardon me?" Eric had spoken to her while she was staring at him as though he was a triple fudge sundae. She watched as he set a skillet on the stove. Elizabeth swallowed. "You mean food. Yes, I'm starved. Thank you."

Not good. Her first thoughts had been how his mouth tasted on hers and how his hands would feel against her bare skin. He reached for the cheese and a carton of eggs in the refrigerator. A smile flickered over his face and she blushed. She was an intelligent woman acting like a besotted teenager.

She collected her jumbled thoughts and walked to the galley. "What can I do to help?"

"First we should change out of these wet clothes."

She stopped breathing as an image of the two of them entwined on his bed weaved through her. She had overheard some of the single female teachers at her school talking about the excitement of jumping into bed with a gorgeous stranger. She had never understood the appeal of giving into such animal instincts. Maybe it was time to reevaluate. She paused and tried to breathe normally.

Eric ordered Rookie to stay in the cabin and reached for Elizabeth's hand, leading her down a short flight of stairs to the stateroom. "Mine will be too large . . ."

She gasped.

Eric turned toward her and then smiled slowly. "My clothes will be too large, but they're clean and dry. There're on a shelf above the bed."

She glanced around the stateroom to distract her from her thoughts. It was decorated in warm earth tones, and although it was small, it had all the conveniences, including a door leading to a bathroom with a built-in shower stall.

Her face was burning. Why was it so hot in here? She did not trust herself to speak. It was confirmed. She did not know how to behave rationally around good-looking men. Elizabeth amended the thought. She did not know how to behave around Eric.

Eric grabbed jeans and a T-shirt and left her alone in the room. She could taste her disappointment. One of her teacher friends claimed she'd read an article that said sex deprivation over long periods of time caused a person to have a mental meltdown. Elizabeth ignored the fact that her teacher friend was always quoting articles no one could confirm were true, but this article, if true, might explain the reason she was behaving so irrationally, allowing her imagination to kick into high gear.

She had visions of Eric and her changing out of their clothes together. He would unbutton her blouse, and his strong hands would graze against her bare skin while she unfastened his tight jeans.

She groaned.

This was not like her. She fingered the bracelet Cassy had given her and wondered if just for once she should rethink the way she viewed life. She was attracted to Eric. He sure seemed attracted to her. What was so wrong in pursuing how she felt?

Because it was out of character, she answered.

Elizabeth concentrated on trying to clear her mind and vowed to stop listening to her teacher friend.

She found the clothes he had indicated and laid her wet ones over a chair to dry. The jeans she rolled up at the waist and cinched with a belt and the shirt she tucked in. She kept telling herself not to think, to just go with her emotions. For once she wanted to find out where the path led instead of buying a road map to play it safe. Her pulse raced and she took a long calming breath, wondering how she was going to get through the next few hours without jumping Eric's bones.

Chapter Nine

The rich aroma of brewing coffee greeted Elizabeth as she returned to the galley, feeling as nervous as a teenager on her first date. Eric was breaking eggs into a large glass bowl and somehow wearing a T-shirt with a sports team spread across the chest and faded blue jeans, he looked ever better than when she had first seen him. Elizabeth decided she was hopeless.

She camouflaged her nervousness with bravado. "What do you think? Do I pass inspection, Captain?"

His eyes widened as he glanced toward her and a smile curled the corners of his mouth. He let out a soft whistle. "You look amazing. Most of my friends like their women in low cut blouses and tight skirts: me, I'm a sucker for a woman wearing casual clothes, preferably mine."

She moved closer, enjoying the way his gaze traveled down the length of her body. She felt feminine and desirable and turned on. "You're just saying that to make me feel less like a wet kitten."

His voice deepened and he winked, touching the tip of her nose with his finger. "Hey, I like the way a wet kitten looks." He poured her a cup of coffee. "When you get to know me better, you'll learn that I never say anything I don't mean. My sister and brother agree that it's one of my more annoying traits."

Elizabeth slid onto a stool and sipped her coffee. "Delicious." She glanced around the room. "Where's Rookie?"

Eric motioned toward the glass door that led out onto the main deck of the boat. Rookie's nose was pressed against the window. "I don't want to have to compete with him for your affections."

"Won't he get cold?"

Eric poured a cup of coffee for himself. "See, that's what I was afraid of. You just met Rookie and already you're more concerned about him than me. I have a terrible time attracting women with that darn dog around."

"Somehow I doubt that." She bit down gently on her lower lip to keep from laughing.

"Let me rephrase that. I have trouble attracting women I'm interested in."

She loved the way his comment made her feel as she glanced in the direction she had last seen Rookie. "He's gone."

Eric finished his coffee. "There's a fancy poodle on one of the sailboats moored a short distance from here. I'm pretty sure that's where he's been hanging out. I told him she was too rich for his blood, but he doesn't listen to me."

Elizabeth laughed and took another sip of coffee. It felt good to talk about something frivolous. Eric was flirting outrageously with her and she was enjoying every minute. From the twinkle in his eyes and his comments she knew he was attracted to her. This felt like verbal foreplay and she intended to savor every moment.

"You mentioned a brother and sister. I'm an only child. What was it like growing up with siblings?"

He reached over and offered her a slice of cheese. The creamy texture melted in her mouth.

"That was yummy," she said. "Can I help?"

He shook his head as though to clear his thoughts and bent over his task of fixing the meal. "Everything is under control. Are you sure you want to know about my family? It's pretty boring stuff."

She really wanted to know how his naked body would feel against hers, but she nodded and reached for another slice of cheese.

Eric shrugged. "Okay, but remember, you asked. A family like mine was a lot like living in the eye of a tornado. You knew there was a storm brewing; the problem was that you didn't know when it would hit. We're also Irish, so that means two things. The first is that we always disagree, and the second is that we'd give our last paycheck to help each other out."

He reached for onions and red and yellow peppers from a drawer in the refrigerator and began dicing them. "What about you? Did you like being an only child?"

Elizabeth finished the last of her coffee and waited until Eric had refilled her cup. "I didn't know anything else."

He leaned toward her. "Another thing. I'm good at is spotting a classic avoidance tactic when I hear one."

She scrunched her nose. "I thought you said you were a professional baseball player, not a psychologist."

He pointed a slice of red pepper in her direction. "I took a few classes in college. I can see by the expression on your face that in your opinion ball players are as dumb as rocks. I admit I had a tutor in high school. She was kind and patient and responsible for giving me the encouragement to apply to college. I wasn't that large in high school and didn't even make the varsity baseball team. Over the summer, I grew. On a lark, I tried out for the baseball team at the University of Washington. That's when coaches starting to take notice. But if it weren't for my high school tutor, I never would have gotten into college." He grinned. "And don't think I've forgotten you're still avoiding the question."

His easy banter and sense of humor had placed a smile on her face she believed was permanent. "Okay, you win. I hated being an only child. There, are you happy?"

"Delirious."

Elizabeth set her cup aside and smothered a laugh. "You're quite good at the whole psychoanalyzing thing."

He winked. "I'm better than good."

Her heart skipped, then threatened to stop altogether. The silence weaved around them as she propped her elbows on the counter again and watched him prepare the meal. She often had overheard people say that with the right person silence could be an aphrodisiac. She hadn't believed them until now.

Eric added the diced onions to the skillet. They sizzled in the pan as he reached for a bowl of grated cheese. He looked over in her direction and smiled. "You're staring."

"Do you mind?"

"Surprisingly, no."

She reached for a sliced green pepper. "What else goes into this feast of yours?"

"Fresh mushroom, rich cream…"

"Cream? Aren't you worried about calories?"

He lifted his shirt, exposing washboard abs. "I'll do a couple hundred extra stomach crunches in the morning." He lowered his shirt. "I like taking chances. Think of it as an adventure."

She was sure her face was as warm as the temperature of the burner under the skillet. The picture of his abs was imprinted on her brain. Adventurous was exactly how she was feeling tonight.

Eric leaned across the counter and fed her another slice of cheese. His thumb brushed her lower lip. On impulse she took his finger into her mouth.

He was so close she could feel his warm breath on her skin. It was like a soft caress. He fed her another slice. His intentions were as clear as his gorgeous eyes. His mouth parted and her decision was made. Just this once she wanted to take a chance.

Elizabeth rose toward him and wound her arms around his neck, pressing her mouth to his. The rush of passion was instant. She was lightheaded. Heat poured over her as his kiss deepened. She may have kissed him first, but he was taking an active role.

He groaned and drew in a deep breath. "Wow." He grinned. "I should go into the rescue business more often."

She held her breath. "We don't know each other very well. This is crazy."

He smiled. "Insane, but what a way to go."

Eric flicked off the switch on the stove and walked around the counter, taking her in his arms. He pulled her closer until their bodies were pressed against each other.

He kissed the tip of her nose. "Did I tell you the best way to enjoy Eggs ala Eric?"

She shook her head slowly.

He kissed the base of her throat. "Naked."

Chapter Ten

Elizabeth's pulse raced and she thought of a hundred reasons why she should call a halt to this before it got out of hand. She corrected herself. It was already out of hand and the crazy part was that she loved the excitement. He had asked her if she was the adventurous type. Maybe just for tonight, she could be. Eric was her exact opposite she thought bemusedly. He had an easy laugh and only thought about living in the moment. Maybe it was true, opposites did attract.

Eric kissed her lightly. "Just as I expected. You taste like strawberries."

Her tongue moistened the corners of her mouth. "It's the lipstick."

"You're not wearing any lipstick or perfume, remember? He caressed her arms and his expression grew serious. "Not that I mind, but why did you kiss me first? Must tell you though, a second later and I would have kissed you. You're the most beautiful creature I've ever," he paused, "almost rescued. And you are kind and patient and…"

She smiled, interrupting. "You can't know all that about me. We just met. Maybe I kissed you first because I've never done anything adventurous or dangerous in my life, and I wanted to know how it felt. I wanted to break some of my own rules."

He winked. "Wow are we different. I always break the rules." A smile crept over his lips. "Well, I'm dying here. How did my kiss stack up with your expectations? Was it dangerous enough for you, say, compared to sky diving or climbing Mount Rainier?"

Elizabeth traced her fingers over his chest, feeling playful. She shrugged. "I can't remember."

Eric moaned in a mock display of pain. "Oh, Beth, you've dealt me a mortal wound. I must be out of practice. My brother and teammates lecture me on that almost daily."

She smiled, liking how deep and sexy his voice sounded when he called her Beth. She had never had a nickname before. Elizabeth suspected her friends considered her too serious for one. Only one other person had ever called her Beth... She pulled away, looking at him, searching his eyes. She knew that color of gray-green. It was the shade of one of the students she had tutored in high school.

She cleared her throat. She took in a gulp of breath to steady her beating heart. What she was thinking was crazy. It could not be the young man from high school. She swallowed. "I really liked what you said about your tutor helping you get into college. I was a tutor in high school."

His eyes crinkled up at the corners as he winked. "I know."

"How do you know that about me? We just met."

"I have a confession. You were my tutor in high school."

Her world spun. "You asked me out for senior prom."

"And you said no."

She smiled slowly as the memories flooded back. "You used to bring me flowers."

He nodded slowly. "I had it bad."

"I wish I had gone with you to prom." She reached up on her tiptoes. "Maybe you should try the kiss again."

"Is that a challenge?"

"Most definitely. A second chance."

"Then this is my lucky day. I love a challenge." Eric leaned toward her. His kiss was feather soft at first, then deeper, spreading warmth and heat to every part of her body. He pulled back. His voice was low and vibrated through her. "Well?"

She took a deep breath and held onto his arms to steady her shaking limbs. Her pulse raced. "Is the boat rocking?"

He cheered. "Yeah. I'm back. How about that kiss?"

"Not bad."

His eyes widened. "Not bad?" He straightened. "Admit it. I rocked your world."

She laughed and wrapped her arms around his neck again. "Well, there was that."

He cheered again, lifting her in his arms and spinning her around slowly.

Elizabeth held onto him: enjoying the thrill of being in his arms. There was a comfortable way about him that made her feel as though she had found a safe harbor, as though she had known him all her life. She wanted to laugh and smile and spin around until she was dizzy, all at the same time.

Eric brought her back to the ground and caressed her cheek. "I've decided you're a mermaid sent to steal my heart and soul."

Feeling bold she slipped her hand under his T-shirt. His heartbeat vibrated against her hand. "I assure you I'm flesh and blood."

"I'm counting on it."

Eric pulled her close against him and kissed her, sending shivers through her body. His kiss deepened and she opened her mouth and felt his tongue against hers. His hand slid under her shirt and cupped her breast as his thumb brushed against her nipple. She shivered again and sighed in pleasure.

Eric removed the belt around her waist and slipped his hand down to cup her bare bottom. She swayed against the length of his hard body. Her breath caught in her throat as she gripped his shoulders with both hands to keep from falling.

Eric whispered against her ear. "You're not wearing any panties."

It was hard to breathe. His hand was caressing her slowly. She did not want him to stop. She closed her eyes. "They were…wet."

"You're still wet." He groaned and kissed her full on the mouth, then drew back and tore off his shirt.

She put her hand on his bare chest. The contact sent warm shivers through her. Her fingers grazed his stomach and moved down. His bare skin jolted her senses. Her heart pounded as she fumbled to unbutton his jeans and slip them down.

Eric unbuttoned her shirt, his fingers caressing her skin; he removed her clothes as though in slow motion.

She wanted him to hurry.

She wanted him to slow down.

Bending over her he kissed her again. This time there was an urgency and hunger that matched her own.

He gathered her in his arms and carried her to the carpet, removing her jeans. Stretching out beside her, he put his hand on her bare stomach. "This feels like a dream. If it is, I don't want to wake up."

Her heart beat so loud it echoed around her. "Neither do I."

Eric leaned toward her and kissed her tenderly. She arched to meet him, wanting to have him deep inside her, wanting this night to last forever, wanting the enchantment to never end.

****

Elizabeth lay on the bed nestled against the length of Eric's hard naked body as morning sunlight streamed through the window, casting warm shadows over the stateroom. Last night they had moved from the floor in the main area to the bed and then in the wee hours of the morning they'd lain exhausted in each other's arms and fallen asleep.

She stretched like a cat, remembering their love-making, and sighed. It had been the most wonderful night of her life.

Eric rolled over and put his arm on her waist as his hand moved lower. She arched against his touch, feeling her senses awaken.

"Again?" she purred.

"Again," he chuckled as his hand moved even lower. "This is how I always imagined it would be between us."

Chapter Eleven

Cassy flicked on the lights in the Second Chance restaurant and drew the lace curtains aside. Last night's rainstorm had swept the streets clean, and the morning light sparkled over the bustling town. She glanced at her watch. They only had an hour to finish sweeping the restaurant and rearranging the furniture before last night's wedding reception.

She was happy with their decision to come here from Ireland. This country was all sparkly and shiny on the outside, as were the people who lived here, but she'd discovered in a short period of time that loneliness was right below the surface. Everyone was so busy regretting what might have been or working toward the future to achieve their material dreams that they had neglected their hearts and the gifts of the present. Her mother and cousins were right. She and her sisters were needed here, and it felt good to be needed, even though true love was forever beyond their own reach.

Cassy took a deep calming breath, appreciating the aromas wafting through the café. The rich smells of cinnamon, nutmeg, fresh baked bread, and brewing coffee coming from Shawna's kitchen made her mouth water. Shawna had outdone herself today. Good thing none of them had to worry about gaining weight.

A loud meow drew her attention. She opened the door. Charmer sat on the threshold, glancing in her direction. Cassy leaned down, picking him up, and laughed. "I wondered when you'd be coming home. You did very well last night with Elizabeth and Eric and have earned an extra treat."

Isadora came up alongside Cassy and petted Charmer under his chin. "When do you think Eric will tell Elizabeth?"

"Tell her what?" Isadora said, bringing over a plate of cinnamon rolls.

"That he has been in love with her since she was his tutor in high school," Cassy said.

"Oh," Isadora said. "So, that's the reason he reacted the way he did when we showed him her picture."

Cassy nodded as she set Charmer down on the floor. "And that's the reason he bought her a ring."

Shawna took one of the rolls from the plate and licked her lips. "It looks like we have another wedding to plan sisters."

Folly Beach

By Darcy Carson

Dedication

*To Heather, Jeremy and Adison Smith for graciously letting
me and mine use their darling beach house at Folly Beach.
It was the inspiration for this story.*

Chapter One

Cicely Brown considered herself a vertebrate paleontologist *extraordinaire*. It wasn't bragging, just simple fact. It took hard work and lots of sweat to succeed in her subdiscipline. No one need know she battled doubts, fears, and was petrified another scientist would challenge her hard work by disputing her statistics.

Which was why she found herself in South Carolina, a short drive from Charleston, at Folly Beach. The six-mile stretch of sandy beach located on Folly Island was considered a hot spot along the Atlantic coastline for discovering megalodon teeth. She was determined to find the biggest, baddest fossilized tooth possible and prove her hypothesis about the ancient shark.

If she could, her career would be secure for life. She could pick and choose which project she wanted to devote her time. Wouldn't that be nice for a change? Not that she didn't appreciate the opportunities offered at Florida State University.

Plus, if she could find a megalodon tooth that wasn't fossilized, this trip might prove her theory that the creatures still existed…a life-time changing discovery.

She sat on the green and white checkered love seat and set up her laptop in the screened-in porch of her rental where a soft breeze stroked her skin. Peace and quiet surrounded her, except for the sound of waves splashing against the shore, the remnants of last night's storm. She'd checked the tide tables and low tide wouldn't be for another hour or so, plenty of time to log into her university account, check her emails, and answer the most pressing, which came from her department head, Professor Rashaad Pringle, an institution by himself.

Afterwards, she sent a text to her best friend, Amy Quackenbush to let her know she'd arrived and settled in. Cicely met Amy in the sixth grade and they clicked right off the bat. Amy was the easiest going person she knew. She always went with the flow. Just don't tease her about her name. Then she went ballistic.

Amy shot an answer back instantly. New puppy. Exhausted.

Cicely smiled and texted back. Are you getting any sleep?

Sleep? What's that?

Cicely laughed. You'll survive. You always do.

Counting on it.

I did warn ya. Talk later.

Next, she headed down the stairs, out the backyard into the bright sunshiny day with puffy white clouds breaking the expanse of blue sky. She carried a water bottle, spade, small rake, nuts for snacks and wore a hat to provide shade from the glaring fall sun. She walked down the narrow street for a block to cross the boardwalk bridge over the dunes next to a bright yellow house and stared at the beach. The beige sand darkened to a slate grey with the receding white froth.

That sea breeze became stronger on the open beach and tugged at her hair pulled back into a ponytail. She yanked the hat she'd impulsively bought at the airport over her ears so it wouldn't fly away and set off toward the water's edge.

The megalodon was the apex predator in his day, the same as sharks were today. Sharks have swum in the oceans for more than four hundred million years. Feared by most, loved by some and hunted by many, sharks were one of the most misunderstood and mysterious creatures to have lived. They'd fascinated her since she was a little girl.

The beach looked deserted. Or almost. No one seemed willing to venture outdoors except for a couple construction men working on beach erosion. They were using a heavy tractor to push sand and football-size rocks into long, straight piles to jut into the ocean.

A sigh of relief slipped out. The most company she would have to endure were pesky oystercatcher birds, especially recognized by their bright reddish-orange beaks. They raced along the water's edge.

After walking the tide line for a while, she selected a spot where the receding water had disturbed the sand and lost herself in digging for shark teeth.

Almost immediately, she found a one-inch, chipped megalodon tooth and stuck it in her pocket, then went back to digging.

A family with two boys and a little girl ran past. The children's excited shouts broke her concentration. She smiled but hoped they continued farther down the beach. Cicely swiped strands of hair out of her eyes and noticed the sun had moved higher in the sky. The day was flying faster than she imagined. She went back to work.

"What'cha doing, ma'am?" asked a male voice from above her.

Cicely glanced up. The man was tall enough to block the sun. He looked like a giant, broad-shoulder and narrow-hipped, even in loose fitting denim bib overalls. He wore no shirt, which exposed bulging, muscular arms. "Excuse me?"

"Sorry, ma'am, I didn't mean to interrupt you. If you're digging a hole, you'll have to refill it or be subject to a fine. I'd hate to see you get into trouble with the *po-lice*. They're pretty strict on enforcing the laws around these parts."

The deep voice with a heavy drawl spiraled through her veins like a warm wave to the tips of her toes. Oh, my. She'd heard of southern accents, but this was her first time of actually hearing a person speak in slow, stressed syllables and they delighted her. She could listen to this construction worker talk all day.

She shook her head and gathered her composure. "I'm searching for shark's teeth."

"Oh, you mean like these." He dug into his baggy overalls and pulled out a perfect specimen nearly the size of his large palm.

Cicely cringed at the teeny-tiny ones tucked in her pocket. She couldn't get a clear picture of the man's face with the sun at his back, but swore he grinned ear-to-ear. Jumping to her feet, she brushed off sand-crusted jeans and black tank top. "Yes. Where'd you find that?"

"Right here. Early this morning. All it takes is a sharp eye, a little effort, and luck. Lots of luck."

She blinked. He had to be kidding. No, his tone implied otherwise. She shaded her eyes, getting her first clear look. Along with rock-solid abs playing peek-a-boo under his bib, he had the brightest, bluest eyes that danced with sensuousness in a deeply tanned face. What a hottie! He made her think of maple syrup on a wintry morning. A gush of delight swept through her chest.

The little birds with the colorful beaks scurried closer to them as they stood still.

She'd always gone for brain over brawn, except this time she was tempted to make an exception. If fair, she'd score him as a twelve on a scale of ten.

"May I?" She reached for the triangular tooth, careful of the serrated edges that were razor-blade sharp.

"Oh sure. I got lots more. Even bigger."

All thoughts of attraction vanished in a heartbeat. Cicely fought the green-eyed monster rising in her core. She kept her calm. The base of the black tooth stuck over the sides of her palm and stretched to the end of her middle finger. It measured close to six inches. The biggest ever found had been seven inches. "Bigger. Really?"

Squeals from the boys who had passed earlier drowned out the sound of the waves. She glanced in their direction where they kicked a ball across the sand, keeping it away from their sister.

As if to confirm his statement, the construction worker pulled a larger tooth from his pocket.

She swallowed hard.

He held one close to eight inches, oblivious to his incredible find. "Between the storm and the work we're doing on the beach, I find between two and five a day. Most are pretty small and broken. I found these this morning. Got a big honker the other day though."

"Bigger than that?" Her heart thudded. "I'm here studying megalodon teeth."

"Megalodon? What's that?"

"It's a gigantic prehistoric shark that was thought to have gone extinct two million years ago. The name is Greek and means 'big tooth'," she couldn't help answering. "You might say it's a sea monster, bigger than a city bus. Most scientist credit it as the precursor to the great white shark."

A steady breeze ruffled the man's sun-streaked hair. "Great whites, huh? We always have reports of them along the coast, especially during migration season in early summer."

Cicely frowned. She was on a timetable. She didn't have time for flights of fancy or chit-chatting, but it wouldn't hurt to be cordial. "I'm Cicely Brown of Florida State University. I've received a grant to study Folly Beach's megalodon teeth."

"Jason Doughtery. Nice to meet you, ma'am. We got loggerhead sea turtles, too. They're on the endangered species list. They usually return to this beach between May and September to lay their eggs. There're special beach watchers just for 'em."

Cicely hated to admit she could listen to the man talk on and on. "You don't say. I'm a vertebrate paleontologist. I study fossils."

"Cool. A scientist." He grinned at her. "You're not originally from Florida, are you?"

****

Jason studied the attractive woman eyeing the tooth he held as if it were the most delicious chocolate bar she'd ever seen. That icy façade started to melt ever so slowly. He grinned to himself. Instinct told him she'd never endured a hot, humid Carolina summer. Too bad. He would have liked to see her clothes dampen and fasten to her svelte body in the sticky temperatures they experienced in the area.

He normally didn't lay on the accent so thick, but something about the ponytailed brunette called for him to do it. She raised a thick-lashed gaze at him and he sucked in a breath. Her lips were full and lush with the hint of pink.

It'd been a while since a pair of lips enticed him.

Most men claimed boobs or legs caught their attention when it came to women. Not him. He rather liked mouths. Shapely, kissable mouths.

The pretty shark lady's brown eyes glazed over every once in a while. Was she interested in hearing about his collection or did she just like him? He couldn't help himself, he hoped it was the latter.

"No, I'm not," she finally answered. "I was raised in Boston. You?"

"Born and bred in South Carolina."

"So, you're local?"

He almost huffed. Born and bred meant local, but kept silent and decided not to correct her. "Charleston is my home town. I'm working with the U.S. Corps of Engineers to maintain the beach here. A mistake was made beyond the breakers that causes severe beach erosion. I don't know the details. The government caused the problem and has to fix it. We started at the beginning of summer and are nearly done."

She pursed her lips. "Hummm, your collection… Could I see it sometime?"

Jason chuckled. "Isn't that a line I should be using on you, ma'am? Inviting you to my place to view my collection?"

A soft crimson blush tinted her high cheeks. "I was going to suggest you bring it to a—a restaurant or a store in town."

Disappointment caught him off guard. Since returning home from his last tour in the army, he'd taken over the family company. He hadn't had time to think about dating. The construction business was booming and he needed to learn every aspect. He'd put his personal life on hold, much to his mother's consternation.

A pelican flew overhead and distracted him for a split second, then he grinned at the woman before him. "Well, ma'am, you sure know how to hurt a man's ego."

"My apologies, Mr. Doughtery," she said stiffly. "That wasn't my intent."

"No offense taken." He tried not to laugh. "And you can call me Jason. Mr. Doughtery is my father."

A fair-sized wave crested near them and forced them to skedaddle higher up the beach to stay dry.

She handed him the shark tooth. Their fingers brushed. An electrical shock swept up his arm and through his body, a jolt of desire that had him clamping his jaw tight. He hadn't felt that strong of a reaction to a woman in ages, if ever.

"I can't help wondering if you play the lottery, Jason. If you don't, you should. Finding large specimens of megalodon teeth is extremely rare. Oh, there's plenty of small ones. All sharks shed their teeth, over thirty-five thousand in their lifetimes. The megalodon lived in the Miocene era and ruled the seas all over the world."

"Then we're pretty lucky it didn't survive." Once again in control of his physical desire, he slipped both teeth back into a pocket. Her gaze focused on the movement as though she hated to see the teeth disappear.

She blinked. "I guess that all depends on your outlook. The megalodon might disagree."

So, the willowy brunette did have a sense of humor. For some odd reason, that pleased him. "True, but I'm pretty sure the surfers wouldn't appreciate running into one."

"Human beings are too small for a full grown megalodon to concern itself with. They hunted much bigger prey—whales, dolphins, squids, and even giant turtles."

"Like the ones protected here?"

She gave him a blank look. "I doubt that. Creatures were plus-sized in the Miocene era. In fact, a few years back, a Carbonemys turtle shell was found in a North Carolina coal mine that measured five feet, eight inches long."

He couldn't help defending the local turtles. "Our loggerheads are the largest hard-shelled turtles in the world."

"That's today. I'm talking about yesterday."

Guilt tried to rise. He should be getting back to work if they were to stay on schedule, except he couldn't stop. He found Cicely Brown delightful. In college he'd joined ROTC and majored in business with a minor in science. His education had been eclectic and varied. Now, he walked a narrow line, acting uninformed, but interested.

Very interested in the woman.

Talking to her had become the highlight of his month. "We seem to have gotten off the track, ma'am. You were asking about my collection."

Rich brown eyes widened. Those tempting lips parted slightly. "You're right, Jason. I don't usually get side-tracked. Shall we set a time to meet and you can show me your specimens?"

He nearly missed what she said after hearing his name roll off her lips for a second time. "Ahhh, sure, if it suits your fancy. There's a really good Mexican restaurant on Center Street, *La Mesa*. Great salsa."

"Mexican, it is then. My treat. When?"

Whoa. This girl moved fast. In all honesty, his male pride preferred making the first move, but this… this was different for a change. "How about Saturday night? Say seven p.m. The majority of summer tourists have gone home. Even so, this is still a tourist town and the weekenders like to eat early. We won't have to fight the crowds if we eat later."

"Sounds good to me."

Her easy agreement pleased him. He grinned at her. "And, you're in the South, ma'am. Around these parts men pick up the tab. It's the gentlemanly thing to do. Can I pick you up?"

She opened that lush mouth of hers, then promptly clamped it shut. "No thanks. I'll just meet you there. Saturday, then."

And with that, Cicely Brown of Florida State University sashayed off the beach, ponytail bouncing, hand clamped on her head, holding an over-sized, floppy hat to keep it from flying off her head.

He hated seeing her go, but enjoyed watching the sexy sway of her backside as she headed toward the bridge that allowed people on and off the beach. It was Thursday. Would she return tomorrow to search for shark teeth?

He nearly flinched as hope exploded like a grenade.

Chapter Two

Whatever made her accept the construction worker's invitation?

Saturday night Cicely felt like a fool standing in front of the mirror in the narrow bathroom of her rental cottage. She'd put on make-up and curled her hair as if going on a date. A real date. That was a laugh.

Her last date had been in college and an utter failure. What was his name? Rodney? Roman? Roy? Damn, she couldn't recall. All she remembered was it had been a disaster. No, that wasn't accurate. It had been a catastrophic fiasco.

Rodney-Roman-Roy had picked her up in a limo. His palms had been wet with sweat and he kept interjecting 'um' between every other word. He'd slicked back his hair with some kind of oily product that smelled like diesel fuel. As soon as she sat in the limo, he had tried to stick his tongue down her throat. She'd jerked her knee into his groin and pushed, hard. He backed off, but seemed upset. She demanded he take her home and, in the ride back, he kept trying to kiss her and cop a feel and she kept rejecting his advances.

Later, the grapevine informed her that he'd been a member of a make-out club and she'd been targeted as the next conquest. Oh, he tried bragging, exaggerating really, about how far he'd gotten with her, but she set him and his friends straight in front of a class they all attended. As far as she knew, the fellow never dared repeat that stunt again.

So why act like this was a special date with the friendly construction worker, a.k.a., Jason Doughtery? Was it really his collection of megalodon teeth? She hadn't even seen it yet. It wasn't like her to become excited without examining the evidence first.

Or could it be the man himself? Was she attracted to him?

Her breath caught at the ridiculous thought. An image of a tanned face with blue eyes the color of the Caribbean Sea, set her heart racing.

She didn't have time for a romantic dalliance with one of the locals, even if tempted to do so. She swallowed hard, dismissing the sudden, unexpected reaction.

She smeared lipstick on, a soft pink shade, and raised an eyebrow. She deemed herself a scientist, a good observer with a mind that preferred analytical and statistical thinking. Of course, it helped to have a healthy curiosity, but attention to detail mattered. She gave herself credit for combining a passion for her work with rigorous ethics, and she would never tire of learning. In her book, making new discoveries counted.

With that rationale, she decided scientific curiosity drove the request to see Jason's collection. It was an opportunity she couldn't let slip through her fingers. If his megalodon teeth were larger than the biggest reported, she had to see them for herself and document them.

And, it didn't hurt that he was easy on the eyes.

****

Jason arrived at *La Mesa* well before his seven p.m. dinner date. One of the things his loving mother drilled into him while growing up was punctuality. Showing up late or tardy equaled bad manners and he agreed. He'd given himself plenty of time for contingencies, mainly heavy traffic congestion, which had worsened over the twelve years he'd served in the military. Fortunately, weekend traffic from Charleston turned out light and he didn't mind driving back to Folly Beach on his day off. This wasn't a date and becoming serious was the last thing on his mind, but he didn't object seeing the pretty scientist again.

Something about her…

He ordered a dark beer, one of his favorites, and sipped it as he munched on chips and salsa. They were as good as he remembered.

People scurried along the sidewalk. The stores usually stayed open for another hour, trying to catch the final sale of the day. He didn't blame the shop owners. The majority of their sales came between April and September. Anything extra was just that—extra.

A flash of movement at the entrance caught his attention and he twisted toward the door of the dimly lit restaurant. There was no mistaking Cicely Brown's lissome figure. He rose to his feet, his chair scraping the uneven tile floor.

She turned at the noise, waved, and hurried over. "Have you been waiting long?" she greeted.

A smile formed automatically. "My whole life, I think."

He held her chair to sit. She laughed and the bubbly sound circled through him in a seductive wave. "I rode my landlord's bike and had to find a place to chain it up."

"You didn't have to worry. Folly Beach has a low crime rate. I checked the statistics when the company won the contract for this job. Didn't want any of our equipment stolen."

"Better safe, than sorry. I'm responsible for the bike. It's a refurbished antique Schwinn that I'm sure is expensive."

A waitress came to the table with menus. "Can I get you anything, miss?"

Cicely eyed his glass and ordered a beer.

Even in a restaurant full of tantalizing aromas originating from the kitchen, a delicate floral scent drew him like a bee to pollen. They were the only patrons. Alone, except for the staff. He rather enjoyed imagining being the last couple in the world as long as it was with Cicely.

"Can we start over? I'm Jason Doughtery… I'd really like to get to know you better. And you are?"

His timing sucked. Before Cicely could answer, the waitress brought Cicely's brew and silently slid it in front of her. Cicely nodded her thanks and took a sip.

"Hmmm. Good," she said, a devilish spark lit her dark brown eyes. "A clean slate, huh? Well, I'll agree if you'll stop calling me ma'am. It makes me feel old. Really old."

"Is darlin' better?"

Jason would have forked over a hundred dollars to take back the words that slipped out. Cicely's expression went from a healthy color to chalk white in a matter of seconds. He was damn lucky she didn't dump her drink in his lap.

He half-stood. "I-I'm sorry. Now, I sound like my Uncle Ben. He calls every pretty woman darlin' or sweetie."

It took several seconds for Cicely's iron grip on her glass to loosen. "Even for women not from here?"

Slow down, boy.

What had his mother tried to drum into his head about women? You had to woo them. They were sensitive creatures. Courtesy counted. Stand when they enter a room. Hold out their chair. Mother called it manners. Women liked sweet words and for a man to listen when they spoke. Except, this wasn't a real date.

"I'm sorry. Really, really sorry. I don't know what's the matter with me. I keep digging myself into a bigger hole, don't I?" He swallowed and sat down. "Take a look at the menu and see if anything tickles your fancy. After we order, I'll show you my collection."

"Last chance, Sweetie Pie," she answered in a nonplused tone as she picked up her menu.

Sweetie Pie. He nearly choked on the words. He didn't argue—no point—when he decided he'd been called worse. A big pressure lifted off his chest. There was more to Cicely Brown than her pretty surface. Something told him she could give as much as she received. Maybe more.

The waitress returned to take their orders.

Afterwards, Jason smiled at Cicely. He scooted his chair closer to the table. "I suppose we should get to what brought you here, huh?"

"That would be nice."

"My collection isn't as big as you might think. Kept replacing the smaller ones as I found bigger and better."

Cicely's eyes widened in surprise or shock. "I hope you didn't throw them in the trash," she said before licking her lips.

His gaze froze on the glistening moisture reflected in the dim light. God, he desperately wanted to kiss her and that threw him for a loop. He had to concentrate, hard. "Ah, no, I gave them to my brother's boys. They like all those dinosaur things."

"Dinosaurs came way before megalodon."

"Afraid I've got a big learning curve when it comes to prehistoric creatures. Maybe you could set me straight."

Cicely smiled in the lull. "That's okay. Most people aren't familiar with the science of paleontology. It is the study of the history of life through fossils. The definition of fossils is the remains of plants, animals, fungi, bacteria, and single-celled living beings that have been replaced by rock material or preserved in rock. Fossils allow paleontologists to understand the different aspects of extinct and living organisms. In simple terms, we combine the skills of a scientist, historian, and detective. Fossils can provide evidence of evolutionary history or organisms."

Jason didn't mind the lecture. He suspected Cicely Brown could make any subject interesting. "It's been a few years, but I recall fragments from a college science class."

"It's a lot to take in. At least you didn't start nodding off."

"If the professor showed as much passion as you do, I might have gone into the field. As it was, I nearly went to sleep. But go on."

"Fair warning… you asked for it. Take whales, for instance. They evolved from land-dwelling animals. Fossils of extinct animals closely related to whales have been found with front limbs like paddles. They even had tiny back limbs." She took a breath and continued. "Studying fossils is not as glamorous as the movies make out. I'm no Indiana Jones or Dr. Grant from Jurassic Park. Besides, my field is considered a subdiscipline."

Jason listened attentively and he wasn't pretending. He'd requested the explanation, so it was only polite to pay attention. "I love your enthusiasm. What got you interested in paleontology?"

She took a sip of her beer before answering, "The glamour, of course. All those movies made it seem exotic, exciting. I can practically quote the entire script from Jurassic Park. But something pulled me to sharks."

"A shark enthusiast. Why?"

"They're fabulous creatures. They haven't evolved in millions of years and I find that intriguing. Not long ago, scientists discovered a Greenland shark they believe is over five hundred years old. That would make a shark the world's oldest living vertebrate."

The woman's excitement was contagious. "Now, you've convinced me that I went into the wrong field. I wonder if it's too late."

"I doubt that. But I bet you're very good at your job. Besides, hunting for megalodon teeth doesn't usually require a lot of skill. Like you said, luck is involved. Speaking of which… Can I see yours?"

He snapped out of his fog. "Oh, sure. Here you go." He lifted the gun-metal grey briefcase he'd brought and opened the locks with a click. He waved his hand over several blackened and/or dark brown triangular teeth.

"Oh my," Cicely gushed. "Do you realize what you found? These are the biggest megalodon teeth I've ever come across. May I?" Her hand hovered over the briefcase. She waited for his nod, then picked up the closest tooth. "This one is nearly six inches long. And this…" She selected another. "It's got to be seven and half inches. Where did you find them?"

A wave of happiness spiraled through him. No explanation existed, but he liked pleasing her. "On Folly Beach."

"Where on the beach? Which specific location?"

"Everywhere."

"When?" Cicely put her elbows on the table and turned the tooth in her hands in slow motion.

The rapid-fire questions reminded him of a debriefing session after a mission. Several lines creased her brow. Intense. He wondered if the pretty scientist even knew she was frowning. "Why the third degree? What's the importance of my teeth?"

Her expression morphed into a smile. "New discoveries are extremely important. Especially ones the caliber of yours. They definitely fall into a category that merits further investigation. Size, of course, is a factor when it comes to fossilized shark teeth. Bigger is better."

Okay, that made sense and she deserved a straight answer. "Almost from the start of construction. The bulldozer exposes them." He gingerly lifted one of the medium-sized teeth from the briefcase. His fingers had been cut by the sharp edges more than once. "I hate to keep showing my ignorance, but what can you tell me about these things? Why are some black and some brown?"

"Megalodons lived some fifteen point nine to two point six million years ago. Their teeth are similar to ours except it has two mineralized structures—a hard shell. In humans it's enamel. In sharks its enameloid and dentin core. As far as color, the fossilization process is the biggest contributor. When the tooth landed on the ocean floor it was covered with mud, silt or sand and minerals seeped into the tooth. Over time those minerals replace the natural tooth to preserve it.

"On the east coast, the most common color is black or grey, but other colors can be found as well.

That usually happens when exposed to the elements or prolonged sunlight. Some colors are rarer than others. This one …" She selected a tooth about four inches long with reddish highlights. "…will command a higher price, even though smaller."

"Guess I never appreciated what I found."

She gave him a smile of approval. "Most scientists believe the megalodon reached a maximum length of fifty-nine feet. A few argue it reached a hundred feet. I'm in that camp."

"Something tells me you like being the underdog. People underestimate you. Right?"

She shrugged and looked away. "Perhaps."

He could read people. It came from needing to make snap decisions in the military. His life had depended upon it. "I bet you're full of knowledge about those sharks."

"As a matter of fact, early civilization used fossils for decorative or religious purposes, even though they didn't understand the significance. Early scholars believed fossils were evidence of mythological creatures such as dragons. In the Middle Ages fossils were regarded as works of the devil. That's not to say some ancient scientists didn't understand their importance. A Greek biologist discovered seashells on land, and deduced that the land was once seafloor. A Chinese scientist used bamboo to form a theory of climate change. Paleontology didn't become popular until the Age of Enlightenment in the 1700s."

Jason maintained eye contact as he listened. "Oh, I get you. Like Darwin. But wasn't he accused of faking his monkey evolutionary theory? Something about combining a human and monkey skull into one."

Voices at the door alerted him to new patrons entering the restaurant. Damn. He preferred having Cicely all to himself.

Her smile pulled him closer. "Accused, but not convicted. In his day, his ideas of heredity were considered outlandish. His theory didn't gain acceptance until he published his *Theory of Evolution*. Although today while the term is popular when referring to modern evolutionary speculation, it is argued by science writers that the term is inappropriate."

Cicely went on, "We've come a long way. In regards to the megalodon, its biting force was ten point eight to eighteen point two tons per square inch. While everything is purely supposition, because of their biting force, megalodons possessed a significantly different hunting style compared to great white sharks. Great whites are known to attack the exposed soft tissues like legs or underbelly. Among my peers, it is believed megalodons went for the tough cartilage of their victims, such as fins. They disabled the swimming ability of their victims, then went in for the kill."

Jason swallowed and grinned. The lady knew her stuff. "Blood-thirsty buggers. Sounds pretty gruesome to me. If you're trying to scare me, you're succeeding. I'm never going in the water again."

Cicely offered a smile. "Even if megalodons lived today, they didn't venture close to shores. You're safe."

"Good to hear," he answered, wondering if he was safe from her.

Chapter Three

Cicely hadn't dumbed down or shortened her explanations. Intuition told her the K.I.S.S. principle—keep it simple, stupid—didn't apply to the man across from her. An innate intelligence oozed from him like sex appeal. Besides, she could never explain her field without using facts. Too much conjecture already existed in the public domain. Supposition butted heads with fact all the time. How else did people come up with their various theories? Most were pure guesswork. Facts lent a measure of truth that gave an air of authenticity.

Pressing back into the wooden chair, it rocked on the uneven tile floor. She studied Jason. To say he looked handsome in jeans and a short-sleeved teal shirt with a button-down collar was a gross under-statement. Well over six feet, there wasn't anything average about him. Maybe it was because she'd already seen those fabulous, rock-solid abs and biceps under-neath his shirt. No guesswork was necessary to imagine what he looked like without clothes. Was touching allowed when they were practically strangers?

Down girl, she told herself. This wasn't a social call.

Cicely reeled herself down and took her own advice. Business first. She inhaled several deep breaths, caught the tangy hint of Jason's aftershave. She smiled at the hot stud sitting across from her.

Maybe it wasn't him.

Maybe his collection excited her. Which, by the way, how many teeth were in the briefcase? She straightened to peer over the top.

"With your permission, I'd like to examine your specimens. If I—I'd like to keep them for some tests," she blurted out, mentally crossing her fingers.

He seemed to study the briefcase, then her, and back to the briefcase. "I guess. If—"

"Thank you," she interrupted, not letting him finish. She didn't want him changing his mind.

He raised his hand. "Will your tests damage the teeth?"

Cicely's heart raced. "Absolutely not! I'll be extremely careful."

He sat and stared at her. "Then, on one condition."

Those words stopped her heart. Like it or not, Cicely would have agreed to nearly anything and swore Jason knew it. "What stipulation?"

"You go out with me again."

"What?" she managed to squeak out. "We aren't really on a date, now."

He pressed a calloused finger against her lips. The touch nearly did her in. It felt as though he stroked her mouth. She gritted her teeth and tried to ignore the sensations driving her insane.

"Is tomorrow too soon?" he asked in that lazy drawl. "Have you toured Charleston? I think you'd enjoy it."

"My research…"

"How about we spend the morning hunting for meg fossils and the afternoon touring Charleston? I'd love to show you my hometown." He cocked an eyebrow as he closed the briefcase and set it on the floor. "It'll take another two weeks to finish our work on the beach. What do you say? Deal?"

He had her cornered. She wanted to study those teeth up close and personal. Needed to really. "How much time will sightseeing take?"

"As much or as little as you want. I warn you, though, Charleston is full of fascinating history. We're not as old as your meg teeth, but we're pretty proud of it."

The waitress brought their meals. "Hot plates. Be careful."

The interruption gave her time to reflect. If she agreed, Jason might gift her one of his pristine, record-breaking samples. If she refused, he might feel insulted that she didn't want to visit his city. She snuck a peek under her lashes. His expression remained impassive, no clue to his inner thoughts. All she knew was that he hadn't actually agreed to let her study the mega-lodon teeth.

"Are there many museums?" she tentatively inquired, still undecided.

Jason beamed a smile at her. "Charleston is full of museums and I'll take that as a yes."

"Do I have a choice?" she asked, taking a bite of food and tasting heaven.

"Always, darlin'."

"I guess a half day of playing tourist won't hurt me. And maybe you could show me where you discovered your teeth. There might be others hidden in the sand." After several bites, she scooted back and laid her napkin on the table. How bad could it be to spend a day in the company of an intelligent, good-looking man?

He hefted the briefcase and set it next to her chair. "Where can I pick you up?"

That question threw a bucket of cold water over her fantasy. Letting a strange man, even a handsome one, know where she lived was out of the question. "How about where we first met near the yellow house next to the boardwalk?"

"Sounds perfect." He picked up his fork and poised it over a platter of enchiladas, rice and beans. "Let's get an early start. Say nine a.m.?"

Cicely nodded slowly, trying to contain her excitement. "Works for me. Thank you. I'll be right back. Which way to the ladies' room?"

Jason indicated a far corner beyond the cash register. She grabbed her purse and headed off.

****

The drive home to Charleston gave Jason plenty of time to mull over the events that transpired with the pretty shark lady. He'd enjoyed himself in spite of receiving a mini history lesson about paleontology. Then, again, he would have listened to her with a sock stuffed in her mouth.

With her being from Florida via Massachusetts meant she wasn't local. He'd heard horror stories regarding long distance relationships… Hold on! He wasn't considering a romantic liaison. He just met her. Friends, maybe.

A wrought-iron gate opened smoothly and he pulled inside the area beside the house that had belonged to his family for generations. He parked and entered through the kitchen. His parents weren't around, which wasn't unusual. His dad liked to tinker on his gadgets in the garage and his mom was probably watching her quiz shows upstairs.

Grabbing a beer out of the fridge, he headed for the den to check out TV. He changed several channels. It didn't take long to discover Saturday night sucked at prime viewing. He almost appreciated having his solitude broken by his father when the tall, lanky man with a full head of white hair strolled into the room.

"You're home early," the older Doughtery said. "What's wrong?"

Jason rubbed a hand over his face. "I've got a lot on my mind. Mostly business."

"Mostly. Hmmm, is that a euphemism for a woman?"

Nothing slow about his dad, and the man always got right to the point. "Don't tell mom."

The elder Doughtery chuckled and claimed his favorite chair, a recliner. "Must be serious. Want to talk about it? Her?"

"Not really, but I will," Jason said, trying to figure out where to start. "I met Cicely on the beach at Folly. I told her about the shark teeth I found and she asked to see them. She acted so excited about them that I couldn't turn her down. Then she caught me off guard and paid the dinner bill tonight, even after I told her I'd pick up the tab."

"Must not be from around these parts."

"Bingo. Originally from Boston, but she lives/works in Florida now."

"A Northerner? Interesting. Not your usual type."

"Not even close, but something about her makes it impossible to stop thinking about her."

"Go with your gut," his father said. "Your instincts have never steered you wrong."

The reminder brought back the memory of a patrol in Afghanistan on the edge of Taliban territory. The operation called for him and his squad to sweep each building in the village. The villagers were either overly friendly or outright hostile. The wide difference in attitude didn't make any sense.

Jason suspected a trap.

When they were about to enter a building, he called a halt. Their so-called informant insisted they continue inside. The man's upper lip crusted with sweat and sand, which raised Jason's suspicions. He ordered the man to go first. Instead, the coward ran off.

Thank heaven he'd listened to his inner voice. A remote check proved the building had been booby trapped.

Jason snapped out of the past. "That's what I was hoping you'd say."

"Since when have you listened to me?" his dad teased.

The steady gait of his mother coming down the hall forced Jason to hold his response.

Tall and slender, with a shiny chestnut bob, his mother appeared in the doorway. "How're my two favorite men? Must be a slow Saturday for the two of you to sit talking. What's up?"

"It's just guy talk, Jill," his dad tried to dissuade.

"Don't feed me a bowl of grits, Ted. The pair of you were whispering. The only time you do that is when you don't want me to hear."

His father tried to look offended. He placed his hand over his heart. "Since when have I kept secrets from you?"

The look his mother tossed his father could cut steel. "Where do you want me to start? Now, what's going on? Are you alright, son?"

Jason cringed. He'd been raised to never lie and considered it a bad habit to start at this stage of his life. "Dad was just giving me some advice."

"Advice? About what?"

Damn, he'd hoped she wouldn't press. He should have known better. "It was nothing."

"He doesn't want to talk about it," his dad said.

A look of genuine worry passed over his mother's face. "He was talking to you. Why can't he tell me, too?"

It might be a long evening, if Jason didn't end it now. Maybe if he gave her a little information she would back off. "You could say it was about another person."

That worried look deepened. "A friend? Not Wally or Bob? They're okay, aren't they?"

"No, Mom. They're fine as far as I know. I met this woman—" The minute he said it, he knew he'd made a tactical error.

Shapely eyebrows arched in a dramatic curve. "A woman? If you found someone you're interested in, I would love to meet her."

"That's a little premature." With a groan, he cast around the room for an escape route. "She doesn't even live here."

His mother approached and blocked him. The hint of jasmine tickled his nose. His mother's favorite perfume. "All the more reason to meet her."

"Don't get any crazy ideas. Nothing will come from it," Jason said.

His mom meant well, but after witnessing the horrors of men crippled or die in war, he'd semi-vowed to never marry. No one he cared for or loved would be put through the loss or grief. Then he went on to give his parents a generic overview of where they met, her occupation, and a brief description.

His mother straightened her tall, slender frame. "She sounds nice and I can hope, can't I? All my friends have grandchildren now to fuss over."

Jason rolled his eyes. "You have grandkids."

"They don't live in Charleston."

"Enough, Mom. You know I chose not to marry while in the army."

"You're not in the military anymore."

An iron resolve gave him the strength to honor the vow he'd made in the army. He never planned on falling in love. "I've only been out six months."

"Long enough to find a steady girlfriend or someone special."

He glanced at his father for help. The older Doughtery suddenly appeared fascinated with the remote he'd snatched off the coffee table. A dead end there. He was on his own. "Mom, I'll give you a detailed report after I show her around Charleston tomorrow."

"You're going to be in town? That settles it. Invite her to Sunday dinner. I'll fix pot roast."

Jason gave up. "All right, I'll ask her…but it'll be up to her. Not me."

****

Cicely secured the briefcase into the basket on the pale green Schwinn after leaving *La Mesa*. The briefcase's weight surprised her. It was far heavier than she expected.

Darkness had fallen but plenty of porchlights gave her a clear view of the road ahead. She rode on the edge of the pavement to avoid any dips, not wanting to jar the briefcase or its precious contents.

Reaching her rental, she dragged the bike onto the porch and flipped on lights as she crossed through the small kitchen. She set the case on the chrome and Formica table and snapped the locks to lift the lid to start her examination of the ancient teeth. She picked up the top one, the tooth with a slight reddish hue. How could one construction worker be so lucky to find such perfect specimens?

As she studied the tooth, her cell phone pinged with an incoming email. A quick glance at the screen revealed the message came from her department head, Professor Pringle. She didn't like responding on her phone.

With a sigh, she left the megalodon samples to retrieve her laptop from the master bedroom and opened the email. No greeting, just right to the point.

It's been three days. Have you made any headway? I expect results. This could make or break your career. Please provide a progress report immediately.

Wow! He wasn't wasting any time. Whose career was really on the line? His? Hers? Probably his. He hadn't ventured into the field work for years. She gathered her thoughts and composed her response.

Professor Pringle,

I am so glad you contacted me. A local man has graciously lent me his collection of megalodon teeth that he recently discovered. I believe it contains several record-breaking samples bigger than the largest ever recorded, which lends credence to my theory that the megalodon reached a hundred feet in size. I plan to document them and will be happy to send you the results.

She hit send and leaned back in her chair. That should satisfy the man. She assumed she had added the right amount of enthusiasm and deference to appease his inflated ego.

Her computer pinged. Professor Pringle again.

I want details, but caution is called for. We must follow proper procedures. How many teeth? What are their measurements? What condition are the specimens in? Send me pictures. Or better yet, send me samples.

Cicely sighed. Maybe she shouldn't have responded so fast. She'd opened a can of worms.

Professor Pringle,

I will be most happy to comply with your requests as soon as I receive permission. Be informed that I just acquired the specimens this evening. These are not mine to send out of the state. The local gave me two weeks to conduct my study. I have not started the documentation process, but as soon as I do, you will be the first I inform.

Hopefully that shut him down.

Wrong again. He shot back a response instantly.

He won't miss one or two.

Cicely reread the single sentence over and over. Her gut clenched and unclenched. All a person possessed was their integrity and she prided herself on being honest. Maybe he was kidding. Yet, she couldn't dismiss the possibility that he meant what he said. He must think her a fool. If repercussions materialized, she knew who would get the blame. Not him. Her.

Professor Pringle,

I can't agree to your request. It's unethical. Removal of even a single megalodon tooth could be construed as theft and we wouldn't want the university or us to be charged with a crime. Think of the publicity.

The man must not have anything to do on a Saturday night for his response popped into her in-box a second after she sent hers.

Don't get caught.

The suggestion infuriated Cicely. She refused to respond and slammed her laptop and the lid on the briefcase closed.

The rapid-fire emails from her department head spoiled the wonderful evening with Jason. Her stomach rolled as if the food she'd eaten had soured in her stomach, which wasn't true. The sick feeling came from Pringle, the prick.

So what if he was head of the grant committee? He had no right to tell her how to spend the money or make the demands he was making on her research. She should report him to the university. She couldn't help wondering if this was the first time he pressured someone to commit an illegal deed.

Chapter Four

Amy facetime me, Cicely texted when she composed herself after the exchange with Pringle. With Amy on the west coast, Cicely let her dictate their communications. It should be early evening in Seattle, but Amy kept a weird schedule.

An instant later her cell rang with an alternating pattern of two notes, E and F, the theme of Jaws.

"What's up?" Amy said, her thick, blonde hair a mass of wild curls hanging in her eyes.

"I met a man."

"Does he have fins?"

Cicely laughed. Amy's outlook on the world and life in general was a little skewed, but that was why Cicely liked her. Amy made her laugh and it would take her mind off Pringle and his underhanded tactics. "No fins, but the packaging is pretty impressive."

"Good on you. Sounds like he might be a distraction. Am I right?"

"Can't afford any right now. No time. My grant isn't large enough to dilly-dally."

Amy shoved her hair out of her eyes with her hand. "I never understood why you had to go to South Carolina to search for shark teeth anyway. Florida has a shitload of those things... Amelia Island, Frenandia Beach, and what about the Peace River? Then there's Manasota Key... Oh, wait. That requires snorkeling and/or diving and you don't like getting in the water."

"I didn't know you were keeping track."

"Excuse me," Amy said, her hazel eyes wide. "Every time I took vacation to see you, you dragged me to those places to hunt for meg teeth."

"I thought you'd enjoy the sights."

A puppy barked in the background. "Shush. Stop that," Amy said, then continued, "I did. I'm just giving you a hard time right now. Let's get back to this man without fins. How'd you meet? Have you slept with him? Give me all the low-down dirty, juicy tidbits."

Nothing shy about Amy. Cicely sighed. She should have expected an interrogation from her friend. "A bit personal, aren't you?"

"So what. Spill. N.O.W."

Cicely questioned the wisdom of discussing men, especially one in particular, but she'd opened this kettle of fish. She would just have to grin and bear it. "Okay. Picture Chris Pine, only younger with a taller Scott Eastwood thrown into the mix."

"I'm drooling," Amy laughed.

Cicely went for broke. "I'm not finished. Now visualize Duane Johnson's muscles. This guy's are just as big and hard looking."

Amy leaned forward until her face filled the screen. "Wait! Wait. Hold it. You've already seen his muscles. Did you ask if you could play touchy-feely? You could call it research."

Cicely blushed at the suggestion. "Amy!"

"What? You've lost your mind if you didn't take advantage."

"A lady doesn't ask to touch a man's muscles." No way would Cicely admit how badly she wanted to caress those amazing muscles. Amy would never let her live it down, if she learned the truth.

The puppy barked again. The picture jerked as Amy moved about her apartment. Cicely caught glimpses of clothes scattered on the floor, and piled on a chair. Her friend still didn't practice housekeeping skills.

"I'm no lady," Amy shouted back, knocking clothes off a chair to settle in a wingback chair she'd inherited from her grandmother. A black puppy of an indeterminate breed wiggled in her lap. "And when did you become one?"

"Oh, he's darling. What's his name?" Cicely asked, trying to sidetrack Amy.

"Samson. No bite!" Amy said before looking at the screen. "Hey, you opened the door on this conversation. You're avoiding talking about Mr. Muscles. That's not fair. Him, I want to hear about. Now."

Not even the puppy's antics detoured Amy. "I give up. We met on Folly Beach. He's a construction worker fixing up the beach. They have a genuine problem with beach erosion and it has to be fixed every few years."

"Boring… Have you slept with him?"

A burst of heat rolled up Cicely's body. She hoped her friend had forgotten that question. "No, I haven't. Nor do I intend to sleep with him. We just met."

"That wouldn't stop me," Amy shot right back.

Cicely shook her head. "Be quiet and listen. Because of his work on the beach, he found several amazing megalodon teeth and I asked to see them. We met at a restaurant and he showed me his collection."

"If he's half as good as you're *not* saying, I wouldn't mind him showing me his collection and more. Much more."

She had intended to use Amy as a distraction from Pringle, not to focus on Jason. "Get your mind out of the gutter."

Amy scratched the fur ball in her lap. "Don't knock it unless you try it. Sometimes my fantasies are all I have to entertain myself with."

Cicely shook her head. "I don't believe that for one minute."

"Hey, you asked me to contact you. What's really up? You okay?"

Amy's tone had softened. Always perceptive, her woo-woo worked very well. Cicely uttered one word, "Pringle."

"That asshole."

"I think he wants me to steal the samples," she answered without thinking.

"Double asshole."

Cicely agreed. "He told me 'not to get caught'."

"Bastard. You're not going to do it, are you?"

"I certainly don't plan to. I just wanted someone else to know what he's really like. You're my touchstone, girlfriend. Sanity in an insane world." To herself, she worried, if Pringle was willing to coerce her into stealing, what else would he demand? She hoped she hadn't put Amy in danger by confiding the gory details. Cicely wished she could take back her words.

In spite of her concern, a smidgeon of relief surfaced. No one would mess with Amy. "Talk to you later. Like I said, I just wanted to get your opinion and hear a friendly voice."

Voice. The minute she uttered the word, Jason's slow drawl rolled through her head. She could have listened to him speak all night. Smiling, she wondered what it would feel like to wake up with his melodious baritone whispering in her ear. Goosebumps erupted on her arms at the crazy thought.

She totally forgot about Pringle.

Delightful images of Jason Doughtery's fit body filled her head. All naked. All different poses.

For a split second, she blamed Amy, then burst out laughing. It wasn't her friend's fault for planting the idea. She did that all by herself.

****

Jason waited in the truck near the yellow house Sunday morning. The minute Cicely mentioned it, he knew the exact dune bridge. He'd driven his dad's pick-up with the locking bed cover because he wasn't sure if she would ride her bike again. As he waited, he deemed the location too remote to leave the Schwinn unattended for an extended period of time. Plus, he didn't approve of Cicely riding home in the dark. Another thing his mother harped on—a gentleman saw a lady to her door.

He spotted her walking in one of the side mirrors and opened the driver-side door to climb out. She must live close. He had a few minutes to admire how black jeans fit her slender legs and the way the dark blouse molded itself to her breasts.

"Hello there," he greeted, giving her a raking glance. "You're wearing good walking shoes. Smart lady."

Cicely beamed at him. "I figured sightseeing involved a lot of walking, so came prepared."

"You're correct. Like I said, Smart lady," he said as her cell pinged. He paused, in case she needed to answer it. She made a face and ignored the call, so they headed over the bridge. After a couple hours they concluded the morning was a bust and cut their beach excursion short. Her phone pinged twice more, but each time she ignored it.

"I was hoping we'd find a blue-ribbon tooth for you," Jason said as he rushed to open the truck's passenger door when they returned to his truck. "Climb in," he said, assisting her, then closing the door.

Hopping in himself, he drove away from Folly Island and headed north to SC 30 E. He figured a little chit-chat would break the ice. "So, Cicely, tell me how you're going to examine my shark teeth."

"Documentation is pretty dry work. Mostly, it amounts to taking measurements of length and thickness. In the world where size counts, fractions are often used. I'll weigh each tooth. Take pictures. Some tracings. If I was in my lab at the university, I would use geochemistry to examine rare carbon and oxygen isotopes in the fossilized teeth. That's a test which allows me to estimate the monster's average body temperature. Thus far, it has been discovered they ran quite hot compared to the great whites and makos of today."

Jason kept his gaze on the road as scenery whizzed past. He was fast discovering, his vow to never marry was developing cracks each time he saw Cicely. He turned left at the fork. The traffic increased.

"Geochemistry, huh? I knew they used it in forensic investigations to gather information on unidentified bodies. How long have they been using it to test for body temperatures?" he asked.

Cicely's soft laughter filled the cab as she peered at him with a steady look. "For years, now. They started using geochemistry in the fifties. But you surprise me. Most non-scientists find what I do pretty boring."

"I'm not most people."

"No, you're not."

Her low voice rippled through him and he spared a quick glance at Cicely as he drove. She cocked her head as she seemed to study him. Something in her rich brown eyes made him squirm under the scrutiny.

Her phone pinged again. "You need to get that?"

Cicely was already glancing at her screen, a frown marring her smooth complexion. He wanted to kiss away that frown.

"No, it can wait," she said, flashing a tight smile.

He went straight on Calhoun Street until turning right onto Meeting Street. It didn't take long before he swung into a three-storied parking garage. "I thought we'd start with a city tour. That'll give you the lay of the land."

Parking on the first floor, he raced around the truck to the passenger side. She jumped down and he laid his hand on Cicely's tiny waist to steady her. He guided her toward a modern building constructed of smoky glass. He blocked the rising sensations exploding inside him over her appealing curves as he headed for the reception desk.

"Hi," he said to the young woman sitting on a high stool behind the counter. "I'm Jason Doughtery. I booked a tour."

"Yes, Mr. Doughtery." She glanced at a piece of paper. "I'll inform your guide of your arrival. You can wait over there. Help yourself to some coffee or water." She indicated an area with couches and chairs.

"Thanks," he answered and escorted Cicely to where directed. "Not sure how long we have to wait. Would you like a cup of coffee or a bottle of water?"

"No thanks." Cicely gave him that introspective glance again. "You had this arranged? What if I said no last night?"

"I'm glad you didn't. I would have been crushed."

His response elicited a smile from her and contentment tickled several pleasure spots on his body. He sensed a good afternoon ahead.

"When did you have time?" she asked.

He couldn't tell if she was upset or pleased. He yearned for the latter. "One of my friends is on the board. I called him last night. He made arrangements."

A second later, a tall skeleton of a man hollered from the far side of the spacious lobby as he rapidly duck-walked over. "Yo! Jason. My man. I thought you were kidding when you asked me to set up a tour. Good thing I followed through."

Jason stood the moment his name boomed across the room. "I never doubted you, Wally, although a little less conspicuousness would be nice."

"Sorry, man. Since when do you need a guide for our glorious city? What's the special occasion?"

"I brought a guest." He indicated Cicely just as her phone beeped again. Thoughts cluttered his mind. Someone wanted to get in touch with her. Was he keeping her from important work? Maybe he shouldn't have insisted she tour Charleston. No, she was an adult, capable of declining on her own. Besides, it was Sunday.

Nor had he forgotten the dinner his mom planned. Would Cicely accept?

She didn't look at her phone, just mouthed, "Sorry. I'll put it on vibrate."

"Cicely Brown, this is one of my oldest and loudest friends, Wally Blankenship."

"Charmed, Miss Brown. Our city is the jewel of the southeast. You'll love it." He looked around. "There's Jessica. She's your guide and one of our best."

A twentyish young woman in a lavender blouse and tan slacks approached them. She gave them a thousand-kilowatt smile and cleared her throat. "Welcome to Charleston. We like to think of our city as a well-preserved Southern belle," she began. "I'd like to head to the city market, which is in the heart of the city. It's our number-one attraction. It stretches four city blocks, all under cover. I'm sure you'll find a souvenir or two at one of the vendors. As we meander the streets, you'll see the various architectural styles of the buildings. Are you ready to begin?"

Jason and Cicely nodded. He shook hands with Wally, anticipating a phone call in his future from his good buddy.

They stepped outside into bright sunshine. Cicely turned to him. He caught her gaze and couldn't keep a straight face. He just had to smile at her. He wanted her to enjoy the day.

"Notice, we don't have a lot of high-rise buildings," Jessica said as she headed for the street corner, "but more than our share of churches, which is where our moniker 'Holy City' comes from. Charleston retains the ambiance of a planation society more than any other city. We have more than fourteen hundred historic structures throughout the city. Many people say our historic district feels like traveling back in time. Just watch your step on the cobblestones. They've been known to twist an ankle or two of the unwary."

Jessica looked at them as if checking on whether they were listening or not. "Keep an eye open for the veranda-fronted mansions," she continued. "After the city market, we'll head for the waterfront park."

Several men turned to stare at them. He stiffened when one man pointed at Cicely, elbowed his companion, then gave a thumb's up.

Oh yeah, that was exactly how he felt. Except he was the lucky one with the drop-dead beautiful woman, and he had no intention of sharing. He reached for her hand and she didn't pull away. That was good because he liked touching her and hoped she returned the sentiment.

After a few blocks, Jessica stopped to peer around at the area. Jason preferred walking fast, but today called for restraint.

"We're not far from the Old Slave Mart Museum," Jessica said. "We can keep going or take a detour to see it."

Jason let Cicely take the lead. She nodded in agreement.

"All right, then," Jessica re-started walking and her spiel, "the museum is set inside the original building that once housed antebellum slave auctions prior to the Civil War, known as Ryan's Slave Mart. The building is believed the last extant slave facility in South Carolina. It's self-guided on two floors with personal accounts via signage and audio exhibits."

The museum was small and had reached maximum occupancy by the time they arrived, which meant they were required to wait outside. Jason scanned the people around them. Most appeared retirement-age couples. When their turn came, they shifted through the throng of people for the next hour, reading signage and looking at enlarged sepia photos.

Jason inhaled a deep breath once outside again, and grinned as Cicely turned to exchange a silent look with him. It felt as if they'd just shared something private. "I remember most of the information from high school, but guess I wasn't paying close attention. My bad."

"It was a lot of data to ingest, but so fascinating," Cicely said, excitement lighting her face. "Some of those old photographs were haunting. So much pain and suffering. Yet the strength those people exhibited to survive is truly amazing."

"I'm glad you liked it," Jessica said. "We're only a few blocks from the Old Exchange and Provost Dungeon. The building was built in 1771 as a commercial exchange and custom house. Today, it is a non-profit historic site. They have costumed guides who tell the history of pirates and patriots once imprisoned there."

"I'm game," Jason said, getting into the spirit of playing tourist. It was as though seeing Charleston in a whole new light. Plus, a sense of pride had developed as his hometown unfolded before Cicely. "Are you getting hungry?"

"Not really," Cicely answered.

Jessica chuckled. "You'll find plenty of samples to eat at the city market."

"Then onward," Jason said.

It didn't take long for them to stop in front of a two-story masonry building painted a creamy tan with white trim and capped with a hipped roof. Jessica handed them tour tickets and excused herself. Jason wasn't going to object to being alone with Cicely.

On the second floor Cicely pointed at the bright turquoise trim separating the cove ceiling and walls. "No wonder you like bright colors. The interior is painted the same as your shirt from yesterday."

"Southerners like colors. In Charleston we can tell Northern tourists because they usually wear dark colors… either black or grey."

Cicely glanced down at the charcoal grey top under her jacket. "Guilty as charged."

They walked around the expansive room and read the placards under portraits of the founding fathers. Afterwards, they went straight to the dungeon where a docent escorted them across the cobblestoned floor from one brick-domed room to another.

"That cell once held Blackbeard," the docent said, indicating a corner sectioned off with iron bars, before moving along and pointing out where a half dozen boxes and kegs were stacked in an area marked munitions. "During the revolutionary war the British used the building as a prisoner-of-war facility. Some one hundred twenty prisoners were held here, although not all in the dungeon."

"This is all so fabulous," Cicely whispered to Jason. "I love history."

And he loved re-hearing the stories with her.

A male mannequin with spectacles perched on his nose was dressed in a shirt with puffy sleeves, burgundy vest, and brown trousers, and sat at a desk. A scarlet parrot perched on a stand and looked over his shoulder. The tour lasted three-quarters of an hour. Jason swore Cicely was absorbing the information like a sponge.

She chuckled softly when they climbed the stairs to the main level. "This place reminds me of Boston. Dad loved taking me and my sisters to museums. The Boston Tea Party Ships and Museum was one of my favorites. I noticed a souvenir shop on the main floor. It's probably like the one at home. Would you mind if I checked it out?"

"Sounds good to me. Maybe I'll find a book on pirates for my nephews."

"That's a really good idea. Maybe I could find something for my dad."

The little store off to the right of the main entrance was stuffed with merchandise. Boxed kits for building sailing ships, stuffed parrots, knick-knacks and shelves displaying books on pirates, Charleston, and sharks.

Cicely began pursuing them like a kid in a candy store. The sight made Jason smile, glad that she enjoyed herself in his city, and that she was with him.

He picked up a book on pirates and one on ships. His nephews were close enough in age that each needed their own book. If they wanted to share that would be up to them. When he selected his two, he turned to find Cicely's arms full of books.

He grinned and she blushed. "Either you can't make up your mind or you like to shop."

"Both," she said, paying for her treasures. "The only way I'll know which books are good is to read them."

"Hey, I'm not judging. Nearly every free minute of mine is spent reading. My current indulgence are thrillers." He didn't ask as he took the heavy sack out of her hands to carry.

They rejoined Jessica and the trio crossed the street to hoof it to a single-storied structure a block wide. He'd visited dozens of times as a teenager. Usually to pick-up girls. Now, he eyeballed the men wandering the center aisle, vigilant for any unwelcomed male advances directed at Cicely.

"Well, here we are," Jessica announced. "Keep your eyes open for our sweetgrass basket ladies. The baskets are considered works of art and I'm sure you'll appreciate their charm. The baskets are only made in South Carolina."

Cicely flicked a beaming glance at him and the sight warmed his heart. Whoa! He swore they were bonding over the day. Was he jumping the gun, making assumptions? No way was that going to happen. This was just one day with a beautiful woman. At least that's what he told himself. "I hope you enjoy this."

"I'm sure I will. Retail therapy is one of my favorite pastimes."

Jason kept his smile to himself. Even if he didn't want this relationship to become serious, he ached to lean forward and kiss her. He just knew his mom was going to approve of Cicely. Her admission that she liked shopping meant she was a woman after his mother's heart.

People milled inside and out of the market. Jason stuck close to Cicely's side and took hold of her hand with his free one. She gave him a quizzical glance and pursed those luscious lips of hers that he ached to kiss.

"I don't want to lose you in this crush," he said.

Chapter Five

Not a chance.

Cicely swallowed, wondering if she'd made the right decision by accepting Jason's invitation to visit Charleston. Not that she wasn't enjoying herself. Playing tourist was the most fun she'd experienced in years, and she relished spending her day with a good-looking man.

She'd buried herself in her work the last few years and hadn't taken time to savor life. It was time. Past time.

A low buzz of voices filled the air. Looking around, she paused. People milled everywhere and the number of vendors with merchandise boggled her mind. "I don't know where to start. I can't even see the end."

"One foot at a time." Jason extended his arm with the sack swaying in his hand. "We're not in any hurry. We have all afternoon. This is for you."

Cicely blew out a long breath. She couldn't remember the last time someone devoted a whole day to just her. The idea humbled her. Her cell continued to vibrate with email messages. Each one from Pringle. After glancing at her screen for the fourth time, she refused to look again.

Jason skimmed a worried look at her, but didn't inquire. He gave her privacy. She appreciated that trait.

In the third building, at a stall with silver earrings and matching pendants, Cicely stopped to admire the jewelry. Amy always bought a piece of jewelry on her trips as a souvenir and the price for these pieces seemed reasonable.

"These are beautiful, delicate looking," she told the salesperson. "The patterns are very unique."

"They're copies of the historic wrought iron gates around the city. Most of the gates were designed by blacksmith Philip Simmons. Pieces of his work have been acquired by the National Museum of American History and others."

"I have a friend who would love a pair, but she only wears posts."

"I can change them to posts."

Cicely looked at the salesperson. "Would you mind?"

"My pleasure." The woman took out her tools when Cicely selected the smaller of the two sizes. Amy preferred small earrings. Cicely kept searching for herself and found one design with swirls enclosed in a circle, and slightly bigger, that she absolutely loved.

"I'll take these for myself. I don't mind hoops."

"That pattern is from the railing on the front of the Old Exchange building down the street," the woman informed her.

Jessica was quick to say, "We just visited there. They'll make a nice memento."

"It's mid-afternoon. Need a break?" Jason asked. "I know I can use one."

Cicely paid for the earrings and tucked the boxes on top of her cell in her purse. It might deaden the annoying vibrations she felt.

"There's a good restaurant across the street," Jessica volunteered. "It's small, but clean and the food is exceptional."

Everyone agreed and Jessica's recommendation proved excellent.

Afterwards, full from lunch, they stood outside the restaurant and looked at the growing crush of humanity filling the market.

Cicely loved shopping, but sometimes crowds got to her. She groaned.

"You okay?" Jason asked, his blue eyes bright with concern.

"Think I've reached my quota of people."

Jason nodded as though he understood. "I'm not much for crowds either. Reminds me of being in the army and on patrol. Always had to be on alert in populated areas."

"Thank you for your service," she responded. It was easy to visualize Jason in the military. She'd seen him scan the crowd while he stood with his posture erect. She suspected he was accustomed to walking much faster, but paced himself for her and Jessica. One thing that pleased her was he didn't have a buzz-cut. She liked how his brownish hair seemed to fall across his brow with sun-bleached highlights.

"We could dash down to the waterfront and explore the park," Jessica suggested. "It's not that far. There we have the option of walking around or taking a water taxi to view the city from a different angle."

The suggestion matched Cicely's mood. "Majority rules. Jason, what would you like to do?"

"Hey, this is all for you, but sometimes less is more."

Cicely cracked a smile. "A man after my own heart. Let's go to the waterfront."

A puzzled expression passed over Jason's face for a split second as Jessica led them away, toward the water. There was no chance to inquire what bothered him. More surprisingly, Cicely couldn't explain why his feelings mattered.

Somehow Jason took the lead with her by his side. Birds cawing alerted her when they drew closer. They walked down a palm tree-lined street, and she spotted a huge fountain in the shape of a pineapple. Tourists queued up to take photos in front of it.

"Sorry about the crowd," Jessica said. "If you want, we'll come back when it's not so busy. Look closely, sometimes you can spot dolphins frolicking near Fleet Landing. Across the bay, do you see that island? That's Fort Sumter, where the first shot in the Civil War was fired."

"You sound like tourists," said a woman behind them. "I couldn't help eavesdropping, but I hope you're enjoying this wonderful city."

Cicely turned. An elderly woman who looked like a stiff breeze would blow her away smiled. Barely five feet tall, she wore a prim, buttoned-up pinkish tweed suit with a white blouse collar peeking from underneath. "Guilty as charged. I'm the tourist, and yes I am loving every charming minute I've been here."

"Excellent. I come here every day. I adore meeting new people. Talking to them. Telling them about Charleston."

Cicely cocked her head, curious. "Every day? You must live close."

"No, hon, I can't afford to live within the city. Too expensive. I drive in. I worked in the city for over fifty years. Once, I was secretary to the longest serving mayor. Oh, the stories I could tell."

Jason stepped forward, the bag of books bumping his leg with the movement. "Lilly Tuttle?"

"Oh my, didn't know anyone still remembered my name."

Jason winked at Cicely, but didn't let the woman see as he turned to her. "You're famous."

Husky, cigarette-damaged laughter tumbled from the grey-haired woman. "You're too kind, flattering me, young man."

The woman was a character and delighted Cicely. "Sounds like you led an exciting life. You should write a book."

A twinkle lit faded hazel eyes. "I have. A real tell-all. I've written it all down with documentation. It's in a downtown bank vault. I can't publish it while I'm still alive. The secrets I know and the lies I can reveal… Politicians' dirty secrets, the mob activities… People would put a hit on me like that." She snapped gnarled fingers with fingernails painted bright red. "My will instructs my granddaughter to take it to a publisher after I'm gone."

Cicely blinked at the woman's answer in amazement. If it was too dangerous for her to print the book, what about her granddaughter's safety? She hoped the family had had a good sit-down discussion.

With a sigh, she couldn't believe how fast the day disappeared and doubted she'd ever experience another as pleasant. As they walked along the cobblestoned road, they passed a row of three-storied houses in a range of pastel colors—yellow, pink, light green, periwinkle, and lavender.

Cicely stopped to admire the houses.

"That's Rainbow Row," Jessica said beside her. "A very iconic sight in the city nowadays. It dates back to 1740. There's an old rumor that drunk sailors landed here and came ashore to paint the houses in various colors. The thought was that they did it so they could remember where they lived. Others claim it was a way to inform people who lived there. No one knows the truth."

"They're delightful," Cicely said. "I think I'm in love with Charleston. I can see why the citizens are proud to show it off."

If Cicely's sense of direction was accurate, they'd made a complete circle to return where they started. After thanking Jessica for being an expert guide, Cicely walked beside Jason to his vehicle. "How much do I owe you for this wonderful day?"

Jason switched the sack to one hand and tucked hers into the crook of his arm. She melted at the sensation of hard muscles under her fingers. The urge to give them a squeeze proved a great temptation.

"This whole day is my treat," Jason answered. "I'm glad you've liked it so far."

"There's more?"

****

"Afraid so," Jason said, lifting Cicely by her trim waist into the truck. This was his first chance to ask Cicely to Sunday dinner. "Orders from my mother. She invited you to dinner tonight."

"Oh, I couldn't impose. Besides, I'm not dressed properly."

"You look fine to me. Better than fine. Mom told me she was making pot roast. Hers is famous. You can't turn her down. She only makes it on special occasions these days. You wouldn't want to disappoint her, would you?"

He shut the door before she answered, hurried around, climbed in, and buckled his seat belt. He knew he was laying it on as thick as his drawl, but didn't want to end the day with Cicely. He could almost see the cogs and wheels whirling in her pretty head. He wondered if she would accept the invitation. Hoped so.

He merged with the traffic. He lived close. She'd have to give him an answer soon.

"Since you put it that way," Cicely began, "I accept with one condition."

Jason's heart stopped. He kept his attention focused on the traffic. "What?"

"Stop at a store where I can run in and get flowers as a hostess gift."

"Okay, darlin'. I'll stop for you, but trust me, you're the best present they'll ever receive."

He pulled into the parking lot of a gas station/market.

Cicely jumped out before he turned off the ignition. "I'll be right back. Stay there."

While he waited, he questioned his motives for bringing a woman home to meet his parents. The action had serious undertones. And he wasn't sure how he felt.

It was as if his pledge to remain single had weakened. Matters were moving way too fast, and he had no idea how to slow them down.

Or, if he wanted to…

Cicely returned a couple minutes later with a bouquet of mixed flowers that filled the cab with a floral perfume.

They spent the few miles to his house talking and laughing about the fun they shared as he drove.

Turning onto his street, the lights on his house lit up the block. He pulled through iron gates where the original carriage house converted into garage stood. Mom was pulling out all stops.

****

Cicely's mouth fell open at the red-brick mansion shooting skyward four stories. It even had a tower. Her gaze flicked between the grand building with verandas stretching across the front and side and Jason.

"This is your parents' house?" she asked, eyeing the divinely handsome man. Moonlight and artificial light caught the defined angles of his face. For a breath-stealing moment, she could only stare and wonder how it would feel to be held in the arms of all that malesness.

She'd endured a pretty long dry spell when it came to sex. Oh, plenty of chances presented themselves. Only she didn't believe in friends with benefits. Being intimate meant more to her than that. Was her reaction to Jason lust or attraction? Her heart raced. No doubt fluttered in her mind—one hundred percent something different. Deeper.

She tightened her hold on the cellophane wrapped flowers as she teetered on the edge of a fantasy. Admitting the feelings calmed her racing heart.

"Mine, too. After being in the army for over a decade, my mother wasn't ready to cut her apron strings and I didn't have the heart to find my own place."

Time seemed to stretch between her reaction and Jason's response. The man was being kind to his mother. Another point in his favor. "You're a good son."

"You want to see the insides of this grand old lady?"

"You bet."

****

Jason loved showing off the French revival house. As a kid he'd never thought twice about living in the huge, old place. All he remembered was running through the halls, his voice echoing.

Now, with delight beaming on Cicely's face, his childhood home made him proud.

"We'll go in the front door for the full effect," he said, leading her on a side path through the garden where rose bushes cast a heady aroma of rose, green tea, honey, and citrus into the air. He knew the exterior with its mansard roof and dormers were hallmarks of opulence of America's Gilded Age. He led her up the stairs.

He opened the outer door with stained glass in the transom and stepped into the foyer filled with no less than five vases full of flowers. A winding staircase sat off to his left. An inlaid floor was half hidden by a blue and red carpet his mother had picked up on one of her shopping excursions.

After Cicely finished taking in the sights, he escorted her to a room with twenty-foot ceilings, a marble fireplace, crystal chandelier, and several seating areas throughout the long room. More vases of flowers added their heady perfume to the air.

"This is the front parlor," he said, gesturing. "My favorite spot is sitting in front of the fireplace to read a book."

"Jason," his mother called, "that better be you and your guest... or I'm going to skin you alive."

His father's laughter followed his mother's footsteps clicking on the hardwood.

"Tour's over. Here come my parents."

"Should I be worried?" Cicely asked, clutching the bouquet to her chest until the cellophane crackled.

"They're going to love you," he said aloud, and to himself, wondering if he was falling for the gorgeous shark lady. Could the right woman make him break his vow? Was Cicely that woman? Only time would tell.

His mother swept into the room, followed by his father. Both were dressed casually. He'd worried she might have gone all formal. He should have known better. His mother was no dummy. She would have realized that sightseeing didn't require fancy clothes and was trying to put Cicely at ease. He'd thank her later.

His mother beamed and he laid a kiss on her forehead before she swept passed him to wrap Cicely in a hug. "Welcome, I'm Jill Doughtery. I'm so glad you accepted my invitation."

"Ted," his father said behind her and stuck out his hand when Cicely was set free. "Nice to meet you."

"Cicely Brown, it's very kind of you to invite me to your home, which is quite spectacular." She held out the flowers. "I brought these, but you seem to have plenty."

"Thank you very much." His mother accepted the bouquet. "I love flowers."

A silent signal passed between his parents and his father disappeared, only to return with a vase that was one of Jason mom's favorite. His mother took a moment to arrange the flowers.

Jason smiled and edged Cicely toward one of the red and yellow floral-patterned sofas in the room. When she sat, his parents claimed the matching one across from it.

His mother started the conversation. "Jason tells me you hunt for megalodon teeth. That you believe those sharks were much larger in size than the current theory."

If Cicely was surprised, she hid it well. "You know about megalodons?"

"Indeed, I do. I'm utterly fascinated with Shark Week, and all those phony shark movies on the Science Fiction channel. Every once in a while a good movie comes out and I'll go by myself if Ted won't accompany me. Most are a bit far-fetched but I don't care. They're fun to watch."

Cicely chuckled. "I think you and I have a lot in common. I adore movies, especially fictionalized ones about sharks. I semi consider myself a cryptozoologist, and it sounds like you're one, too."

"I'm not familiar with that word," Jill said, leaning forward, a fascinated look on her face.

"It's actually a pseudoscience and subculture. People who believe that extinct or mythical creatures might still be alive. You know, big foot, yeti, mermaids, Nessie."

His mother's eyes widened with a look of excitement. "The Loch Ness… Oh, Ted, our next vacation should be to Scotland."

"Yes, Sweetie. Whatever you want," his father answered with a twinkle in his eyes. "Science and science fiction is quite a combination. From what I've heard about the academic world, it's a tough place to survive."

Cicely stiffened as though his father hit a nerve. It was so fast Jason wondered what was going on. Was she worried about her job? A demanding boyfriend? Jason's gut tightened at the thought.

"I try not to think about it," she said.

His father nodded. "How do you separate the two?"

Jason leaned back and let his parents talk with Cicely while he enjoyed the view.

Cicely flicked him a glance as if checking on him. He shrugged and she grinned. They'd done so a dozen times during the day as if sharing a secret and each time he swore their bond grew stronger.

"It's easier than you might think," Cicely began. "You sort out the facts. Research is complicated, but if documented properly and communicated clearly, the truth will shine through. While Hollywood creates entertaining movies, reality always trumps fiction. No creditable scientist can issue unsubstantiated statements without suffering the consequences. Their reputations are at stake."

His dad put his hand on his mother's knee. "Same as the construction business. Or any business, for that matter. A good reputation is golden. It can make the difference between winning a contract or not."

His mother patted his dad's hand as they exchanged a look and stood. They'd always been openly affectionate with each other.

"Are you ready to eat?" his mother asked. "I hope you brought your appetite."

Cicely chuckled as she rose, refusing to confess they'd eaten a big lunch at mid-afternoon. "All the walking we did today built up mine. I'm starved. Is there anything I can do to help?"

"Nothing at all. Everything is on the table."

His mother crooked her arm into Cicely's and they moved into the dining room. Jason stayed at Cicely's side and his father trailed behind.

Cicely's mouth dropped open as they entered the dining room with a coffered ceiling. Candles lined the center of the table and fluttered as they disturbed the air finding their chairs. A bas-relief cornice above the main window depicted a three-masted sailing vessel, emblematic of the original owner's business.

Jason shook his head. His mother had brought out the best china. Crystal glasses sparkled. Silver-domed platters were strategically placed on the table.

Aromas of pot roast, potatoes, and carrots curled into the air. His mouth watered.

"Ted, pass the pot roast to our guest," his mother announced before turning and smiling at Cicely.

In the brief moment of quiet, Jason said, "We met Lilly Tuttle."

His dad paused, arms outstretched. "Oh, my God, she's still alive? She's part of Charleston's history. Her family dates to the first settlers."

"I wonder what her secrets are…" Cicely accepted the platter from his dad. "It makes for a good mystery."

"It's probably pretty explosive. I imagine there are families who hope she lives forever," his mother added with a smile. "Speaking of family… Tell me about yourself, your family. Jason says you're originally from Boston."

Jason cringed. "Mom!"

"It's all right, Jason," Cicely answered, patting his hand. "She's curious, is all. I've nothing to hide. I'm the oldest of three sisters. My mother died of breast cancer when I was twelve. Dad raised us and I think he did a pretty good job."

In spite of her answer, a deep sadness came and went in Cicely's eyes. She tried to bury it, but Jason saw it, heard it in her voice. He would have done anything to eliminate the sorrow.

His mother stopped passing bowls of food to his father. "Oh, I'm terribly sorry. I didn't mean to remind you of a sad event. Please, forgive me."

"I'm used to telling people. Being the oldest I remember the best, but my sisters were only seven and three, so they constantly asked questions about her. What was she like? What did she look like? My middle sister, Kara, was particularly curious. She remembered faint images, but over time the details have faded. It was hard on her, especially when she married a couple years ago and had a baby. My youngest sister, Julie, was just too small to remember much."

"That's so sad," Jill said. "At least, they have you to help keep her memory alive."

Jason tried to change the subject. "Maybe we should talk about something else."

Cicely smiled at him. "It's okay."

Not to him. Anything that hurt her, bothered him. He wondered if he should inquire when they were alone. For the moment, all he could do was hand Cicely a huge bowl of salad and she passed the pot roast platter to him. "So, you're an auntie. I'm an uncle. My older brother, Jake, has two kids, both boys."

The smile Cicely gifted him brightened the room. "Where is he?"

"Jake moved to Texas over a decade ago. He didn't like living in hurricane country. Claimed it wasn't safe here."

Jason tasted his first bite and paused eating at the look of surprise on Cicely's face.

"He left Charleston because of hurricanes?" she asked. "But Texas has tornados."

"Thank you very much, Cicely. That's what I told Jake," his mother answered. "But he refused to listen. And now that he has children, he's putting my grandkids into danger."

"Mom, you and Dad fly to see them almost every other month," Jason interjected.

His mother narrowed her gaze. "That's not enough. I want to see them every chance I can. Children grow so fast, and I want to enjoy them before they become teenagers. All my friends tell me that it's a horrible age, when kids think they know everything and every adult is stupid."

"My dad certainly enjoys my sister's baby," Cicely said "I've never seen him happier."

Jason groaned. "Cicely, please, stop. That's exactly what she wants to hear."

Smiling, she said, "Oh, something tells me you've had a lot of practice handling your mom."

His mother's laughter echoed in the room. "You've figured him out. A lot of people never do."

His mother had no filter, which proved frustrating at times. Still, Jason wondered what Cicely thought of him, his family, and longed to ask her if she approved.

Chapter Six

Jason cringed as the two women talked. Both women glowed. He suspected his grand plan to remain single were crumbling fast, and he wasn't sure how to react.

"I have an extra-special dessert in honor of our guest," his mother broke the silence. "You mentioned Cicely was from Boston, so I thought I'd make her feel at home and made Boston Cream Pie, though why they call cake a pie is beyond me."

"It is strange, isn't it?" Cicely answered with a smile as wide as the Grand Canyon. "All I can tell you is that it was created in the mid-nineteenth century and remember reading pie tins were more common than cake pans. Still, it's one of my favorites and I haven't had any for ages. I'm sure yours is delicious."

Jason's mother shot him a smug look before turning back to Cicely. "You be the judge. Meanwhile, did you know that Boston and Charleston are somewhat sister-cities?" At Cicely's shake of her head, his mother went on, "At one time wealthy Charlestonians made Boston their summer home while Charleston became Bostonians winter home."

He loved watching Cicely interact with his mother. They seemed to click with each other and reminded him of a matched pair of bookends.

At a signal from his mother, his dad stood and started clearing the dirty dishes.

Cicely rose, gathered her plate and reached for his.

"You sit down, missy. You're our guest," his dad said. "That's my job. In this house, the person who didn't do the cooking, does the clean-up. It's only fair. Right, Jill?"

"Yes, dear," his mother answered before stepping toward the long sideboard to pick up a domed cake platter. She set it on the table, removed the top, then returned to the sideboard for four small plates and sliced into the cream cake.

"I'll lend you a hand, Dad," Jason volunteered and his father didn't object.

"Well?" Jason asked in the kitchen, knowing his father was dying to speak. "What do you think of Cicely?"

"Besides being drop dead gorgeous, just like your mom at her age. Who, by the way, is still good looking in my eyes. I'm always amazed she picked me."

"You're avoiding my question, Dad."

"No, I'm not. I have no qualms bragging about your mom. I got damn lucky with her. And I think you feel the same about Cicely. She's pretty, smart and… well, nice. If you're asking for my blessing, you have it."

The comment set Jason on his heels. Damn, he wasn't even sure of his own motives. Parents must have a built-in radar when it came to their children.

After he and his father finished clearing the table and loading the dishwasher, they returned to the dining room and sat down to plates of Boston cream pie and freshly brewed coffee.

Looking at Cicely, one thing Jason knew, he didn't want the night to end.

****

Cicely broke her own rule and let Jason drive her to her front door. She rationalized her actions because she'd met his parents. Sitting in the truck's cab, she discovered she liked being alone with Jason.

"Thank you for the wonderful day and evening. Charleston was delightful and your parents… They're charming. You're really lucky. I wish I could cook like your mother, but I'm afraid that'll never happen."

"If you want lessons, she'd be thrilled to teach you. It's one of her passions."

Cicely's breath hitched. His suggestion reminded her how precious time in Folly Beach was and dimmed her good mood. "I'm sorry. I'm only here for two weeks, and with your samples to study, I won't have much time left over."

Disappointment sped over Jason's face so fast she thought she imagined it. She fumbled for the door handle. He sprang into action and came around to open it for her. He took her hand with his and molded his other one to her waist as she hopped down. Heat ignited sparks shooting through her body.

When he retrieved the bag of books from the truck's bed, the neighbor's porchlight came on. She imagined the noise alerted them to the activity and they peeked out their window. Racing up the solitary step to the porch, her outdoor light popped on with the motion. She unlocked the door.

"Thanks again for a wonderful day," she said, meaning it.

"You're welcome, darlin'. I had fun, too."

Her insides melted at the endearment. In fact, if she were honest with herself, she'd been looking forward to hearing him call her darlin'. It was cute the way he dropped the 'g'.

A car with its high beams on traveled down the street under the speed limit.

Cicely watched it roll by, then turned to Jason. "Maybe I'll see you on the beach."

A smile formed on Jason's face and she swore he wanted to kiss her. The thought warmed her heart. What a nice way to end the day.

Maybe she should kiss him. Surely, a quick peck on the check was an innocent thank you for the marvel-ous day. The temptation to take the initiative swelled in her. It wasn't like her to drag events out. She'd always been a person of action.

She licked her lips in anticipation.

****

Jason's heart spiked at the moisture glistening on her lips. He edged closer and planted both hands against the house on either side of her head. Leaning in, he inhaled a bouquet of flowers that smelled a hundred times better than the full vases at home. A steamy burst of desire cluttered his mind. He longed to kiss her. Dreamed about it all day.

"Cicely," he said.

She tilted her chin at his whisper. Her brown eyes glittered under the porch light. "Yes?"

Their lips were inches apart. Her sweet, warm breath caressed his face. Those wondrous lips were so close. The top lip slightly bigger than the bottom one. He visualized nibbling on it at his leisure.

Jason stroked a finger down the side of her face. Her loose hair brushed the back of his hand and fires of desire erupted. When he cupped the back of her neck and pulled her toward him, a shiver rumbled through her body.

There was no better time to kiss her and he did. Her lush lips softened beneath his and his heart leapt with joy. He didn't maintain the kiss for long. Kept it short and sweet. It was one of his rules. A first kiss should be a tease left as a memory. Just long enough to create fantasies and short enough to make Cicely eager for him to kiss her again.

And he would. Soon.

Oh, yeah. And that was a promise he vowed to never break.

Her arms dropped to her sides when he stepped back. She caught her lower lip with her teeth. The urge to move in and hold her tight against his chest nearly overwhelmed him, but he didn't want to pressure her. Slow and easy was his motto concerning Cicely.

"'Til next time," he said softly, and held his breath as he headed for the truck.

A shoe scuffed behind him as if she followed. "Jason."

He stopped and turned. "Yes."

"Would you like my phone number?"

His heart raced. Call him an idiot. That kiss must have thrown him off. He should have asked first. "You bet."

She dug into her purse where she'd stashed her cell under the jewelry boxes. They exchanged numbers and he controlled the impulse to kiss her again.

"Thank you," Cicely said.

"Back at cha, darlin'."

With those words, Jason jumped into the truck with the biggest grin on his face and drove off. Best day ever.

****

Cicely stood, stunned. When the red glow of taillights on Jason's truck disappeared, she opened the door to the rental and collapsed against it. Squeezing her eyes closed, the memory of the gleam in Jason's cerulean blue eyes drew her in, and she imagined the passion awaiting her in his arms.

She feared walking across the floor, afraid her knees would buckle. Her insides had turned to mush at the touch of Jason's warm lips on her mouth. Had he noticed how she'd stretched to her tip-toes and started to encircle her arms around his shoulders just as he broke the kiss? How embarrassing. Up close, his aftershave, a hint of orange, cinnamon, nutmeg and wood had intoxicated her. She thought she'd died and gone to heaven.

Could anything come from this relationship? Probably not, but it still was a tempting idea. Jason Doughtery could easily turn her life topsy-turvy.

Regaining her composure, she glanced at her phone. The sight on her screen burst her balloon.

Twelve emails from her boss. Ridiculous. The man was over-reacting. The number was well over what a rationale person would send. She began reading them from first to last.

1. This discovery of large megalodon teeth is very exciting. I wish I was there assisting you.

2. Any results?

3. Details are imperative.

4. Why haven't you responded?

5. Contact me.

Cicely stared at the last message. Was that an order? It certainly sounded demanding and matched the egotistical professor. Pringle could ruin her career. While she didn't want to, she started reading again.

6. I'm sure you're deep into your analysis. How many teeth have you inspected?

7. Send details.

8. What's the matter? Why aren't you responding?

The tone changed to a whine. A bit surprising for the professor. After all, the man was accustomed to getting what he wanted. Her heart sped up. The next email could say she was fired. She needed her job.

9. I'm becoming concerned. Why haven't I heard from you? Is everything all right?

Another change. And fast. She swore he sounded anxious. What did he have to worry about? Had something happened at the university?

10. This is important. It is vital that you keep me informed.

11. As your superior, you are obligated to report your progress. You wouldn't want to jeopardize your career.

Ah, threats. That was more what she expected. Yet for some odd reason, it didn't bother her. Interesting. Knowing Pringle, the threat was legitimate. He blessed all the associate professors hirings and firings.

She almost laughed. She hated office politics. If her career wasn't on the line, she would have channeled Amy and shot back a snarky response. Her friend would call this a shitty night. What was going on in Florida?

She read the final email.

12. Cicely, I've demonstrated extreme patience waiting to hear from you. A discovery of this importance must be handled with great care. Someone with experience and impeccable credentials should be in charge.

Now, she understood. It was all about him. She should have guessed.

What did surprise her, however, was that he actually addressed her by name. Normally the professor needed prompting when it came to remembering someone's name. Maybe the discovery that might change the history of megalodons had made him desperate. A desperate person was dangerous.

She mulled over various scenarios. Had he been hasty and leaked information about the find? It caught someone's attention and now the university pressured him for evidence? She tried to give Pringle the benefit of doubt. He could be caught between a rock and hard place.

Pringle was tenured. He did not have to worry about being fired with or without cause. She did. Her situation was precarious.

The temptation to let the man stew proved alluring.

Chapter Seven

The familiar theme of Jaws blared from Cicely's phone at the crack of dawn. She squeezed her eyes shut, praying the music would stop. It didn't. When she finally peeked at the screen, the area code came from Florida—the university's main number.

"Hello," she said sleepily.

"Cicely, thank heaven I've reached you. I've been worried sick something terrible happened to you. It's unlike you to not respond immediately."

Pringle.

She glanced at the clock on the nightstand. It glowed green in the dimness, showing seven-thirty am. "Professor Pringle, I'm fine."

"What a relief. Where were you yesterday? Why didn't you respond to my emails?"

Scooting up in the bed, she wished for coffee. "I'm so sorry. My phone died yesterday and I wasn't in a position to charge it."

"I find that hard to believe."

The lie she made up caused her to wince, but his sarcasm irritated. "As soon as I had enough power, I did text you. Didn't you receive it?"

"I did not!" he snapped. "Did you leave the samples? I bet you did. Why weren't you studying them? Where were you? How could you be so irresponsible and leave those priceless teeth? I gave you more credit than that. What if they'd been stolen?"

He was jumping to assumptions. Except, he'd been right. His voice had risen several octaves. Almost a panic mode. This version of her old professor was not the man she remembered. She needed to craft her answers with care. "They were safe."

A huff of disgust sounded on the line. "You were my prize student. I trained you better than that! You can't guarantee their safety when you leave them unattended. But as long as you vouch for them now, that's good." He paused. "Umm, I don't mean to pressure you, but when can I expect samples? It's vital that I corroborate your findings, you know."

Cicely hit the speaker button and climbed out of bed. It would be impossible to go back to sleep now. She threw on the jeans she wore the last time on the beach. "Look, professor, my plan is to spend today documenting the samples. I'll be thorough. You can depend on me."

No comment from the profession. He used silence as a weapon and made her wait several long seconds before answering. "Of course you will, Cicely. It's just that I'm very excited about the discovery of these teeth and especially since they're so much larger than anything ever found. If they're not fake or reproductions… Think of the ramifications. I've already started drafting an article for publication in the Scientific Journal."

What? Wait. What article?

Oh, Pringle was correct—publication was the next step. The saying in the academic world was publish or perish. But usually years of verification happened first.

Cicely scowled as she headed for the kitchen to fix coffee. "Professor, that's moving forward awfully fast. We don't want to be presumptuous. Accuracy counts. I'm not—"

"Of course. Of course," he interrupted in a condescending tone. "You're absolutely correct. Authentication must be substantiated. Under my guidance, I have the utmost confidence the results will be accepted without doubt."

The dig hurt. She buried the twinge. No use letting the odious man get under her skin.

She made the coffee and waited for the pot to beep when done. Cicely grabbed a mug, poured herself a steaming cup of black coffee and sank into a chair at the kitchen table. That first sip infused caffeine into her blood stream.

"I'm not sure how long certification will take," she said, swallowing another mouthful.

"A lot is at stake. Reputations. Careers. I expect you to devote the rest of your time at Folly Beach validating the teeth. As I've already said, you could send one of the samples to me…Or better yet, a record breaking one. I promise to return it before anyone notices it missing."

She stopped cold. How dare he? She would notice. If Pringle didn't possess morals, she did. What guarantee did she have that he'd return the teeth? His word? Ha! She was having serious doubts that once he got his greedy hands on them, the rightful owner—Jason—would ever see them again.

She started to sit at the kitchen table, but moved to the sofa. Her conscience obligated her to keep Jason informed the whereabouts of his megalodon teeth.

Her phone pinged with an incoming call. *Jason Doughtery.* Her heart jumped. He was calling on his way to the job site. She paused and considered terminating the call with her department head. In the end, she let Pringle rattle on with his bombastic narrative.

"What's your timetable, Professor?"

"The Third International Conference will be held in Madrid next May. I'll contact the event coordinator, he's an old friend, to schedule a workshop into the program. I'd like the article to appear in the journal the month before. Drop a few hints in the right ears. Stir up interest. It'll draw the biggest crowds to the workshop."

By his tone, Cicely's intuition screamed that the workshop wasn't going to be a panel. No, he plotted a one man show, going for all the glory. Cringing, she wondered, what her next step should be.

She finished her coffee, and poured a second cup. Gritting her teeth, she strived to maintain a pleasant tone. "Thanks, Professor. That gives me an idea of how much time I have to research these teeth. Guess I'd better get busy."

"Ah, oh, right. I can't stress the importance of keeping me informed. Daily."

When he hung up, she pounded her head on the table. Not good. Not good at all. She ignored the fact that he was stabbing her in the back. What had Amy called him—double asshole. The description fit to a 'T'.

She needed to clear her head. Grabbing a light jacket, she stormed outside. The briny scent of ocean invigorated her. Walking was a good stress reliever.

Then she eyed the pale green Schwinn. She could take a bike ride. A bit of exercise would relieve the stress. No. Better yet. She'd go shopping. The stores would be open by the time she got to town. If not, she'd treat herself to a latte and wait. A little retail therapy to make her forget about Pringle.

Her actions might be construed as avoidance, but she didn't care. Just call her Queen of Denial.

****

Midday, under a warm sun, Jason spied Cicely walking toward him on the beach carrying a brown paper bag. His spirits lifted. He wiped sweat from his brow. Why hadn't she accepted his call when he'd rung her earlier in the morning? Worry had flared that after one date, she might have had enough of him. His gut rolled at the thought. His call had been innocent enough, to let her know they were making better progress than he'd originally scheduled. The job for the Army Corps of Engineers would be complete at the end of the week.

Waves lapped the shore with the incoming tide. The sound drowning the noisy calls of red-beaked oystercatcher birds that raced along the water's edge.

He two-stepped toward her in the loose sand. That floppy hat of hers was going to blow away in the brisk wind. He'd buy her another one, if that happened.

"Hey, there," she said, coming to a stop in front of him. "Glad I found you."

"Me, too. I had a great time yesterday."

"Me, too."

Jason smiled at her identical reply. They'd done so last night, too. He wondered what else they had in common or if she noticed. His attraction to Cicely could not be denied and he wondered if a long-distance relationship would work for them. Was it wrong to wonder if any chance existed that her feelings were mutual?

"I didn't expect to see you today," he said. "Figured my samples would keep you busy."

A teenage couple holding hands walked along the beach. They nodded in passing. The sight made him want to sweep Cicely into his arms and kiss her silly. Wiser judgement kept him from doing so.

"I'm heading back as soon as I give you this... For your mom and dad. As a thank you. It's a bottle of Cabernet and a book about sharks that I bought at the Provost Museum."

Jason ignored the cawing of seagulls. He just stared at the brown paper bag Cicely held out to him. "Oh, I swear you're going to be my mom's new best friend."

"She's easy to like. Your father, too."

He jammed his hands in overall pockets to keep from reaching out and burying them in her shiny brown hair. "I'll be sure to tell them you approve. They certainly approve of you. They were waiting up for me when I got home to give me the third degree."

The sun heated his bare back and arms as he stood facing Cicely. He swore freckles dotted the bridge of her nose. The overwhelming temptation to gather her into his arms nearly did him in.

She laughed. "Your parents are sweet. I'm sure they have your best interests at heart."

"I'm a big boy and can take care of myself." To himself, nothing was going to stop him from continuing to see the sexy shark scientist for as long as she remained in Folly Beach. "I have a favor to ask."

Cicely arched a shapely brow.

He swallowed and nodded at the bag she held. "Can I pick up my parents' gift after work? I wouldn't want to break it on the job."

An expression he couldn't identify flashed over her face. Refusal. Acceptance. He held his breath until she answered. "That's fine with me. As a matter of fact, why don't you stay for dinner? While my cooking can't hold a candle to your mom's, I can throw together a pot of spaghetti and salad. What do you say?"

His heart raced and he leapt at the invitation. "What can I bring?"

Her thick lashes fluttered. "Absolutely nothing, except your wonderful self."

Warmth spiraled through him at her response. Beaming at her, he ached for his work day to end. "I always keep a spare set of clean clothes in my vehicle. If I could use your bathroom to change into them, I'd be grateful. Besides, I doubt you want me tracking sand inside your place."

"Sure. Okay. I better get going. I've got lots of little parts to pull together. See you this evening."

Jason couldn't believe his good fortune. Dinner three nights in a row with Cicely. He was one lucky man.

****

Cicely walked on air all the way home. She never expected Jason to accept her impromptu offer, but was thrilled he had. She must be insane. She didn't know what possessed her to invite him to dinner. Seeing him on the beach just proved too tempting.

At her rental, she stashed the wine and book on the counter, then sat at the kitchen table to compose a grocery list. Fifteen minutes later she pedaled to the local market as fast as her legs could pump.

When she returned home with her basket of groceries, she put the meat on simmer and began tidying up the place. She eyed Jason's grey briefcase with a moment's regret. She hadn't even given the megalodon teeth a cursory examination. That wasn't like her. Jason was proving quite a distraction.

Was she wasting time when she should be concentrating on studying the teeth?

Probably. But she didn't care.

What if she explained that her department head wanted to analyze them, to substantiate her findings? All it took was a simple request to fulfill Pringle's demands.

Maybe inviting Jason to dinner would solve her problem. Kill two birds with one stone.

She stomped her foot. No second-guessing. That wasn't why she invited him.

She genuinely liked his company. Asking him to dinner had nothing to do with Pringle. Nor was she one of those women attracted to men because of their powerful positions. Jason was as smart, if not smarter, than any of them. Of course, it didn't hurt that he was drop-dead good-looking. She wanted to spend time with him because she liked him.

She tried to reason it logically. First, his megalodon teeth drew her, but somehow an emotional connection had developed.

Oh, God. She rolled her eyes. Had the conversation with Amy planted licentious ideas in her head, and they were spreading like weeds to manipulate her?

Cicely shoved the wicked thoughts away and kept herself busy until the early local news came on television. That was her cue to make herself presentable. She freshened up, changing into black slacks and a light-weight black and brown sweater.

The aroma of garlic and tomato sauce packed the rental's interior. She put cheese bread in the oven to warm. Everything was in readiness. All she waited for was Jason's arrival.

As she puttered in the kitchen, a knock rattled the door. Her heart skipped a beat. She hurried to answer the summons.

Jason stood in the growing darkness. He smiled and warmth mushroomed through her.

"I brought you these," he said, holding out a bouquet of pink carnations, deeper pink freckled lilies and a few red roses. The heady scent of cloves, an ethereal lemony scent, and the unique fragrance of roses preceded him. "I'm assuming you like a variety of flowers, because that's what you bought my mom."

"I do, with carnations as my favorite, but you didn't have to bring me flowers."

"I wanted to."

No words expressed her appreciation for his kindness. Something told her being nice came naturally to him. She accepted his gift and pressed her nose into the bouquet. "Thank you. They're beautiful. Come in. Come in."

He stomped on the outdoor mat to knock off the worst of the sand and stepped over the threshold. "Just like you, darlin'."

She edged backwards, flushing with embarrassment. The combination of compliments and his slow drawl curled through her veins in a deep tease. She would never tire of listening to him speak. She wondered what it would be like to spend the rest of her life with him. That thought jolted her.

Swallowing, she composed herself, then noticed his bundle of clothes. She pointed to a middle door along the wall. "There's the bathroom. If you'd like to shower, you're welcome to use it. The towels on the rack are clean."

He stepped forward, only to stop and peer over his shoulder. "You're sure you don't mind."

"I wouldn't have offered if I wasn't sincere. In the meantime, I'll put these in a vase."

Cicely turned to rummage through a cupboard. Floorboards squeaked as Jason headed to the bathroom. Within seconds water gushed from pipes. It took a herculean effort not to visualize him stripping off his overalls, stepping into the shower, scrubbing those hard muscles clean.

She shook her head. Stop that! She didn't daydream, especially about men. Even handsome ones with killer smiles.

Ten minutes later the bathroom door opened, and steam billowed out. Jason stood under the lintel in jeans and a green polo shirt, his hair slicked back, rubbing his jaw. "I should have brought a razor."

She laughed, genuinely pleased. "You look fine. I'll toss your overalls into the washer."

"You don't have to do that."

"It's no problem. Might as well clean them while we eat." She indicated the table. "Sit down. Everything is ready."

"It smells delicious," he said, remaining standing. "But first, do you have a broom? Afraid a lot of sand dropped on the floor."

"It's tucked next to the washer."

"Great. I'll sweep up my mess."

He closed the door and she carried the bubbling pot of spaghetti to the table and set it on a trivet. When she lifted the lid, the aroma of onion, tomato and bell peppers rose. Returning to the stove, she pulled foil-wrapped bread from the oven, then grabbed a salad from the refrigerator. As she unwrapped the bread from its container the scent of melted parmesan wafted in the air. She licked her lips in anticipation of eating.

Jason stepped out of the bathroom with a dust pan. He stopped and stared at her for a moment as if in a trance. Then he seemed to shake off his fascination, saying, "Garbage?"

She pointed under the sink, dashing into the bathroom before he could object to toss his work clothes into the washer. She returned and sat down. "Sorry, but I forgot the wine."

He put the broom and dustpan back in their original location and joined her. "What about the wine you got for my parents?"

"That's for them."

A wicked gleam shown in his blue eyes. "What they don't know, won't hurt them."

"You're bad, Jason Doughtery," she teased, thinking, *so bad, you're good*.

His grin lit up the small kitchen. "I'll replace it."

"Well, it is a red, and that goes with dinner. I guess it's okay."

She jumped up to grab a wine opener from a drawer, and passed it and the bottle to Jason to do the honors. Her fingers tingled as she set them into his large, warm hands. He popped the cork and filled their glasses half-way.

They sipped at the same time, both nodding approvingly at the earthy flavors with a hint of berries. A nice way to start the evening.

Cicely watched Jason eat fast, like a starving man, devouring two he-man sized servings. When he stopped, he pushed his chair back and patted his stomach. "Tasty."

Never considering herself a good cook, Cicely blushed. "I'm glad you approve."

"You have hidden talents. That tops my mom's spaghetti."

Standing, Cicely tried to decide whether or not to clear the table or do it later. Later was better she decided on the spot. "Afraid I forgot dessert. Would you like to sit on the porch and finish the wine? It's nice to listen to the waves in the dark."

Jason's grin beamed at her. "Being alone with you is the best dessert."

"Thanks," she answered, going to the porch and settling on the checkered love seat to sip her wine.

Jason sank down beside her. "Cicely," he spoke softly. "I'm giving you fair warning, this evening is not going to end without me kissing you."

An almost giddy sensation zoomed through her. Her imagination went wild. She set her glass on the coffee table and turned toward him, prepared for anything. His glass clinked hers as his followed suit, then he lifted her chin with his finger. Warm steel traced the side of her face and she couldn't help leaning into the contact.

"You're so pretty," Jason said, his breath feathering over her skin a second before he gathered her into his arms and soft lips caught her mouth in a searing kiss.

Seconds. Minutes. Cicely lost track of time. Didn't care. Never wanted him to stop.

When he pulled back, she inhaled a deep breath. "You're a very accomplished kisser."

Soft laughter rumbled up Jason's chest. "All thanks to my partner. Kissing you is really easy."

To lend credence to his words, he peppered her face and neck with kisses. The soft scent of soap wrapped around her as easily as Jason's arms. She grabbed another deep breath, unable to think, except for reacting to the fantastic sensations Jason created. He respected her privacy, was easy to talk with. She felt safe with him, like she'd known him for years instead of days.

When he gathered her in his arms, she felt herself melt. She'd never experienced that sensation with another man. He nuzzled her neck, then his lips found a ticklish spot behind her ear. While he never stopped kissing her, his hand roamed down her arm and moved to cup her breast in a gentle massage.

There was no stopping or controlling the arousal blooming inside her.

Cicely broke the contact, gasping for air. She pointed inside. "My…my bedroom is the first door."

Jason scooped her up into his arms and carried her like a bride.

Chapter Eight

Early morning sun allowed filtered light into the master bedroom through the curtains. Cicely stretched slowly, contented. The room was quiet except for Jason's soft breathing beside her. He'd stayed the night at her invitation and she wasn't sorry. Watching him sleep for a moment, she thought *'nice'*.

She touched her mouth with her fingers. Her lips were slightly swollen from all the marvelous kissing. The long draught of sexless nights was over, and she couldn't be happier. Jason had made her feel wonderful, a woman desired by a man.

Struggling to slip out of bed without disturbing him, her bare feet tingled on the cool floor. Jason's pants and polo shirt were neatly folded on a chair. He was neat. Another trait worthy of admiration as far as she was concerned.

She padded her way to the bathroom without the floor creaking. A flash of guilt surfaced as she flicked a glance at the kitchen. She'd totally forgotten about cleaning the mess. Or putting Jason's work clothes into the dryer, which she promptly did.

A soft knock against the door startled her.

"Tell me where the coffee is and I'll put a pot on." Jason said through the door, his slow drawl stroking her insides the same way his hands had her body the night before.

Heat rolled through her at the memory. "In the cupboard next to the fridge," she answered, glancing at the wild-haired image in the mirror. What a sight! She scared herself and did not want to do the same to him the first thing in the morning.

Combing her hair and brushing her teeth, she listened to Jason putter about in the kitchen, opening cupboards and drawers, turning water on. She rather liked the sound of having him around to wake up to.

When she stepped out of the bathroom, Jason waited for her. He scooped her in his arms and gave her a quick kiss. When he stepped back, her eyes bulged at the sparkling kitchen. "You didn't have to do that."

He shrugged, gracing her with a boyish grin. "House rule. The cook doesn't clean up the mess."

Laughing, Cicely locked her arms around his waist. "You're a keeper." She nuzzled his neck, gave him a peck on the cheek, and brushed her fingertips over his scruffy face. "Afraid all I have for breakfast is cereal."

"My favorite breakfast food."

The enjoyable moment was ruined when her cell blasted the room with the dramatic theme of Jaws. All it took was a quick glance at the cell's surface to recognize the number.

"Sorry, the university is calling. Afraid I have to take this." She moved away from Jason's warm body. "Hello."

"Well, what have you discovered about those megalodon teeth," Pringle asked without preamble.

The department head's voice turned her blood to ice. Her gaze swept over the open space of the rental. Thankfully, she'd taken measurements of the two smaller teeth. "I've examined two—a four- and six-inch specimen. They were in perfect condition. One has a slight reddish hue. The other is black. Typical for the Atlantic coast. The reddish one actually weighs more than the standard one. That's slightly abnormal. I've photographed them and will send you the pictures along with the data."

"Excellent work. How many teeth total?"

She waited a moment. His constant grilling about her progress was beginning to grate on her nerves. "To be honest, I haven't reached the bottom of the briefcase."

Jason claimed a chair at the table. He cocked a brow.

She smiled at him as way of apology and sat on the sofa.

Pringle continued. "You should do a preliminary check of all the samples. It is best you follow my instructions. You owe me."

"Owe you?" She gritted her teeth until her jaw ached.

Flicking a glance at Jason, a subtle change transformed his expression. She would have sworn it darkened.

"Yes. You would never have received your position at Florida without me vouching for you. And, now that you've made this discovery, you seem to be rebelling. Remember insubordination is grounds for dismissal."

"Professor, that's not tr—"

"Don't pretend you haven't defied me," he interrupted. "Just keep defying me and see where that gets you."

Cicely gasped. Her heart raced. "What's that supposed to mean?"

"I don't have to explain my connotation to you. You know damn well what it means."

"You asked me to steal!"

Jason's gaze arrowed into her. Embarrassed, she lowered her voice, not wanting him to overhear any more of the troubling conversation.

"You're over-reacting. I merely wanted you to borrow those samples for a short while. You should be in full agreement. Receiving a second confirmation from someone with my qualifications will prove your thesis about megalodons being larger than the accepted size without question. After I inspect them, you'll have my full backing. I don't understand your unwillingness to cooperate."

Of course, he didn't understand. "Really, Professor. Are you sure you're not seeking the glory that this discovery will bring?"

"How dare you! Are you accusing me of trying to take credit for this find?"

"Only if you are?"

A grumbling bluster came over the phone. "You can't be serious."

"I've had a lot on my mind, Professor. I understand how important this discovery is to paleontology world and to you."

"I don't need to prove myself. My reputation was made decades ago."

Cicely couldn't continue. Not with Jason sitting feet away. "We'll sit down and have an in-depth discussion when I return to the university."

A rustling came over the phone. "I'm sorry to say this, Cicely, but the reason I'm pressuring you so hard is…because your job is at stake. I hated to mention this, but the university is instituting a thirty percent cut-back. Heads higher than me put your name on the list as one of the associate professors to let go. That's why I've been adamant about verifying your discovery. If true, something of this magnitude will put a feather in your cap and the university's. They wouldn't dare let you go once the world learns of your discovery. It's the main reason I've been so unwavering about examining these teeth."

A lie if she ever heard one. He was trying to manipulate her. Anger made her tremble. She knew damn well he planned to take the credit. "I'm sorry, too, Professor Pringle, but I need to think. You've given me plenty to consider about my future. I have to go." She managed to speak without screaming, and she meant every word.

What was more important? The discovery of the megalodon teeth or Jason's happiness?

Cicely freed a deep, shuddering breath and punched the off button.

****

Jason would have preferred not to eavesdrop on the one-sided conversation. Worse, he hated the haunted look that swept over Cicely's face. The urge to protect her exploded with a force of a bomb. More notably, he wanted to wrap her in his arms and protect her against the woes of the world. If that meant commitment, he was all for it.

"Who was that?" he asked, trying to keep his cool. He didn't have a clue about what was going on and had no right to invade her life.

She blushed. "My boss."

"Excuse my French, but he sounds like a prick."

Cicely beamed. "That's what I call him, too. Pringle, the prick."

The smile on Cicely's face meant the world to him. If some far away prick was pressuring her, Jason vowed to do whatever it took to make it right. He remembered thinking how difficult remote relationships were and decided she was worth the effort. She'd become important to him. He didn't want her to leave… Ever.

"Talk to me. Is there anything I can do?" he asked, wrapping her shaking body in his arms.

She leaned into him and laid her head on his chest. The protectiveness swelling within him became a colossal tsunami, and her show of trust made him feel like he could defeat a monster. "Not really. It's something I have to deal with."

"Cicely, I'm here for you. It might ease your burden if you tell me the facts."

"I don't want to bore you."

"Nothing you say will bore me. Let me help."

As he spoke, Jason realized he meant every word. In less than a week, Cicely had become the center of his life. He led her to the pillow-covered sofa and urged her to sit. When she did, moist tears glistened in her brown eyes. Whatever was at the core of this problem, greatly troubled her.

She exhaled a deep sigh. "You're a nice man, Jason. I didn't mean to involve you in my troubles."

"Hey, I asked. Now tell me. Maybe together we can solve it." He took her hands and raised them to his lips. A quick kiss to each knuckle had Cicely leaning her head down.

"You're at the core," she began, then dropped her gaze.

His gut wrenched. "Me?"

"I'm afraid so. Or, to clarify, your megalodon teeth. I informed my department head of their existence, telling him they were larger than any known examples and he asked… No, demanded that I send him one or two without informing you. In my book that's stealing. My dad raised my sisters and me to never lie, steal or do anything immoral. My whole life is based on those principles."

Jason sat, stunned. The more information he gained about Cicely, the more he realized she was the right woman for him. She had character, was an intelligent, caring woman. Not to mention easy on the eyes.

"Sounds like Professor Prick has a problem, not you," he said, still digesting the information about her boss.

"I knew he was an egotistical, glory-seeking professor, but I never thought he was dishonest. He trained me, was my sponsor on several projects. Signed off the grant that got me here. I trusted him."

Jason listened, fearing a deeper attachment existed. "Do you love him?"

"Love?" Cicely's face reddened. "Good God! No. Not in the way you're suggesting. He's my grandfather's age. I wouldn't be surprised if that's why he's so determined to get his hands on your teeth. He wants one last discovery stamped with his name on it and add to the list of his achievements. He was quite a celebrity when younger. Reporters seldom come around to interview him nowadays."

Relief exploded at hearing the explanation. Jason didn't know what he would have done or how he would have reacted if she'd admitted affection for the unknown man. "Why didn't you do as he requested?"

"Because they weren't mine. They belong to you. Stealing is not who I am."

Jason closed his eyes, remembering the magic of the previous night. His vow to never marry had been shattered to smithereens and now he refused to go on without laying his cards on the table. "If I have to choose between you and those silly teeth, it's an easy decision. You can have them. Do whatever you want with them. Give them away. Destroy them. I don't care. You're the most precious thing in my life."

She batted her thick lashes. "I appreciate your offer, but it's become a matter of principle. I'm not sure I can work with or for a person who advocates theft."

"But your career…"

"Is important to me, but not as important as my ethics. This incident makes me question being a paleontologist. If it's this cut-throat, maybe I don't belong in the scientific world. I've survived ridicule for believing megalodons were larger than the accepted premise. I even envisioned they might still exist. I joked about being a looney-tune cryptozoologist, but maybe it's true."

He grinned. "Be whatever you want. You pegged my mom as one the other night and I think you're correct. You two would make a good team."

She pulled back a bit to stare at him. A smile lifted her lush mouth at the corners. "That's a good idea. I might benefit the field. At least I have a science background. Most cryptozoologists don't."

Jason sat on the edge of the sofa and pulled Cicely with him. As he did, he held her sweet body close. "I don't care who you are. What you are. Only you matter."

A sense of fulfillment crammed his mind as he sorted his feelings. His emotions ran high from weeks, months, maybe years, of restraint. With Cicely, he could free them all. His pledge to remain single no longer mattered. She was a woman worthy of being loved, heart and soul, and he was just the man to do it.

Chapter Nine

After Jason left for work, the day dragged and didn't seem as bright, even though the sun shone beyond the windows.

Cicely harbored no interest in analyzing the shark teeth. That was a first. Her work had always taken priority. She'd spent a decade speculating on the megalodon's size, its very existence. The ocean was a vast unexplored place. No one could predict the incredible discoveries yet to be found.

What was she going to do?

There had to be more to life than megalodon teeth or obnoxious professors.

She sank into a kitchen chair and let the metal's coldness seep into her body. When she lifted her head, sunshine pierced the bow window, and glass figurines sparkled on the sill.

Was that a sign? Of what? Should she call Pringle and apologize or just submit her resignation? So many choices.

She paused, mulling over various scenarios. Being Queen of Denial came easily. She put aside making a decision and elected to go shopping. She hadn't really taken time to check out Folly Beach's stores and she was in the mood for something different.

Riding the Schwinn into town, the people working in their yards smiled or waved. Most of the shops were tourist traps with glitzy knick-knacks, t-shirts, and rows of beachy items. She by-passed them. One apparel shop had several swimsuits on display in the window. She dismounted and went inside.

Swimsuits of all different colors filled the racks— white, blues, pinks, oranges, and prints with dozens of patterns. The store even had a small shoe section in the back. Mostly sandals.

Nothing grabbed her attention, so she left.

Bella Beach, the other women's apparel store was across the street, sandwiched between a pizza shop and Chinese restaurant. Cicely headed in its direction. It contained summer dresses and tops.

One blouse, in particular, caught her eye. A linen coral-colored blouse that buttoned up the front with a sweetheart neckline. She never wore bright colors, but this one appealed to an inner sense. She bought it without even trying on and tucked her treasure into the basket to pedal back to the rental.

Once home, she changed clothes and loved how the vibrant color put a bloom on her cheeks. Maybe Southerners knew something Northerners didn't. Adding colors to her wardrobe would be high on her list from now on.

Then, she opened Jason's briefcase and began removing the megalodon teeth, only to jerk to a stop. Squeezed in the bottom of the grey interior was a tooth that matched the color exactly, which made it nearly invisible. It filled the entire length of the briefcase, at least fifteen inches. Her fingers trembled as her hand hovered over it.

If the largest fossilized tooth recorded was seven inches and the consensus among her peers was that megalodons were fifty-nine feet, this blew their hypothesis to pieces and validated her theory that the creatures were over a hundred feet in length.

She sat gaping at the discovery of a lifetime. And felt nothing. Oh, a brief moment of euphoria had burst inside her, then zilch. Why wasn't she more excited? Instead of doing a happy dance, or shouting to the rooftop, she shook her head. What was she going to do?

She picked up her cell and punched Jason's number. It rang twice.

"Hello, Cicely. This is a pleasant surprise," his deep voice answered.

Cicely swallowed. She adored hearing him use her name as much as darlin'. "I finally reached the bottom of your briefcase and found that—that honker you mentioned. You weren't kidding, Jason. If I use this in my research, it's going to shatter all the records."

"Do what you want. All I care about is making you happy."

"Will you stop by after work tonight? I think we need to talk."

A chuckle preceded his response. "Sure thing. I'll bring dinner. Chinese okay with you?"

After hanging up, Cicely sighed. The scientist in her wanted to study the megalodon tooth. The woman in her would rather wax fancy about Jason. It was a quandary she never expected to find herself in.

Maybe the truth lay somewhere between the two.

That insight lifted a smidgeon of her anxiety. She put newspaper down and laid the colossal tooth on it and got to work. It measured a full fifteen inches. Using the bathroom scale, not an altogether accurate source, showed the tooth weighed seven pounds. She shook her head in amazement.

One thing she knew for sure…

A media storm would erupt once the world learned of this discovery. Her life would become hectic. Never the same. She would be compelled to travel from continent to continent to lecture at universities, and scientific conferences. Her days would be packed with speaking engagements, papers would have to written, and published.

And so would Jason's.

More importantly, he would lose his prized possession if she cited the tooth as the basis for her announcement. Pictures would never satisfy other scientists. They would demand the right to inspect the specimen in person. That wasn't fair to him.

Would he care? He'd already claimed he didn't. But was that true?

Cicely jumped when a knock on the door broke the silence. A quick glance out the kitchen window showed it was still daylight out.

She rushed to the door to find Jason standing on the porch, holding a large plastic bag.

"You're early," she said, happy to see him. "I didn't expect you until after dark."

A boyish grin materialized on his face, making those blue eyes of his sparkle like blue sapphires. "I couldn't wait to see you, darlin'," he said, setting his burden on the table, edging the teeth aside and grabbing her in a bear hug. He kissed her until her concerns became a memory.

Breaking the kiss, he glanced at the ancient shark teeth scattered over the kitchen table, then back at her. "You look fabulous. I like the new blouse."

She laughed, loving his compliments. "How'd you know it's new?"

"Maybe I have a sixth sense…"

The twinkle in his eyes raised a cluster of suspicious. Jason appeared too pleased with himself. She narrowed her gaze. "I doubt that. Now, spill."

He wrapped her in his arms again. "I stopped to pick up our dinner order and the owner of Bella Beach ran into me. She mentioned you were in."

Cicely knocked him lightly on the chest. "That's not fair."

"Yes, it is… Because I picked these up for you." He held out a small square box.

At his urging, Cicely opened it. A pair of coral earrings, an exact match to the blouse, were nestled inside. Cicely's heart burst. "They're gorgeous."

"Not as gorgeous as you."

She dashed to the mirror in the bathroom to put the earrings on. Who ever thought a pair of earrings could thrill her so much?

Off to the side, Jason looked around. "You've been busy."

"Not really." She turned to face him, cocking her head. She hoped he didn't think she'd spent the day working on the megalodon teeth. "Let's eat on the porch."

"Whatever makes you happy. We can eat right out of the containers."

Cicely laughed. This was a side of Jason she hadn't seen before and she approved of his laid-back attitude. She grabbed forks and napkins on the way out.

They sat together on the patterned love seat, eating and exchanging containers until full. Afterwards, she leaned back against Jason's chest. The steady rhythm of his heart relaxed Cicely. Maybe an academic career wasn't for her? Maybe that tingle she felt was her biological clock ticking. It was a real possibility. Although not a romantic notion, her feelings could be hormones wanting a family. A husband. Children.

A life Jason could provide.

As if he knew her thoughts, he said, "Cicely, I like you. More than like… I care about you."

"I feel the same about you."

"Oh, hell. I love you. I want to marry you. I want you here with me. Or, I'll go wherever you want." He let out a loud breath. "There I said it."

Genuine happiness curled through her veins in warm streams. "We think alike, Sweetie Pie."

Slipping off the love seat, he went down on a knee. He took her hands in his, kissed them as he looked up at her. "Will you marry me? I haven't gotten a ring, but maybe we could pick one out together."

"Yes, yes, I'll marry you."

****

By the time they finished eating, darkness was starting to fall.

"Let's take a walk on the beach." Jason pulled Cicely into his arms. He was thrilled she'd accepted his proposal. He'd heard the rental was due to come on the market in the near future and he made a mental note to buy it. It would make the perfect wedding present for Cicely.

She sent him a smile that kicked his heart into a fast pitter-patter. "Where we first met. I'd like that."

They took the stairs down to the backyard and cut across the grass.

Jason held Cicely's hand in his. His callouses had thickened since working on the beach and he hoped she didn't mind the roughness. "You have to go back to Florida?"

She squeezed his hand. "Only to resign."

He stopped on the street. "Are you sure?"

"I can't work for Pringle. I'd rather not work than associate with a thief."

Jason pressed his lips together. The code of honor matched his own.

Down the block they crossed the boardwalk bridge over the dune. Lights in other houses began to shine out the windows.

The side of the yellow house glowed golden in the last vestiges of the day. Looking up and down the beach, no one else was present. It belonged to them. Both smiled at the other in a silent communication.

Jason led Cicely to the water's edge and put his arm around her waist. She wrapped hers around him and leaned against his side. It felt right for them to stand and catch the sunset gleaming on the calm water. Dusk was his favorite time of the day and nothing was better than watching the last of the sun's rays' dip into the water with someone he cared about.

Seagulls circled overhead and pelicans flew toward the pier for roosting as the light faded. An inner peace filled him as he soaked up the view. He could go to sleep tonight with hope that tomorrow would be a better day, one of the thousands he could share with Cicely.

"Do you think megalodons are out there?" he asked.

"I do. There are a lot of challenges in understanding megalodons. The most abundant fossils are their teeth and they disappeared from the fossil records about two point six million years ago. A few agree there's only a one percent chance that they're still alive."

"I have the utmost confidence that if they're out there, you'll find them."

"It's a real long shot. Seventy-one percent of the Earth's surface is covered in water and it extends to depths of thirty-six thousand two hundred feet. Ninety-seven percent of that water is in the oceans. Alleged sightings all over the world keep the legend alive. Most marine biologists and shark researchers tell us its impossible. Until there is scientific basis like a fresh megalodon tooth or documented sighting or some other form of proof is presented, I doubt I'll ever be able to prove my theory."

He embraced her tighter to his body. "Hey, one percent is better than nothing. Never give up, Cicely. I believe in you and love you with all my heart."

"Double that," she answered him, rising on her tiptoes to give him a kiss.

****

Well beyond the breakers where the waves smoothed out, a silent killer with a twenty-foot high silver-grey fin knifed through the water.

The End

Vines to Water

By DeeAnna Galbraith

Dedication

To Kyle and Amy Johnson
of Purple Star Wines
Thank you

Chapter One

Cady St. Simon scanned the dirt road that divided her parents' vineyard from the vineyard at Silver Vines, and ended on the bank of the Yakima River. She loved this place and the unplanted space at the end of the road. Cady called it her beach.

She breathed a sigh. It was the end of April and both vineyards had sprouting leaves and buds, but that's where the similarity ended. Silver Vines would grow grapes, which, with the right processing, would be the basis for some of the best cabernet sauvignon in the country. And they could have been hers if her parents hadn't been outbid when that vineyard had gone up for sale. Sold to a newcomer to the area. A sneaky buyer from North Carolina who came in at the last minute. The sale was a done deal, but she couldn't help mourning the loss of the grapes and the beautiful wine she could have made with them. So close.

She hadn't met the new owner yet, but Mr. Penn Abbott had been busy. She'd heard he'd introduced himself to the members of the local American Viticultural Area (AVA) Alliance. Probably sucking up.

Deep-throated barking interrupted her thoughts as a huge dog came charging down the dirt road. Panic lit her insides. Fitted with a saddle, the shaggy giant could be ridden by her jockey-sized miniature pinscher, Desi. Luckily, Des wasn't with her. Outrunning the oncoming beast was out of the question. Cady narrowed her eyes, and unwilling to fully face her own destruction, held her arms straight, palms facing out. The big dog came in sideways, knocking into her shins and flattening her like a bowling pin.

Covered in road dust and unable to escape, the dog added insult to injury by pinning her with a massive paw and licking her face.

"Kraken!" a man yelled and yanked the dog off by its collar.

Swiping at her face, Cady looked up to see a tall, blond stranger holding the dog's head steady and forcing it to focus as he made a bobbing motion with his fist. The dog sat, but strained to look back at her without success. Her attention was then drawn to a pretty woman with a light brown ponytail, holding her hand across her mouth in an effort to hold in a laugh.

Cady sat up as the man gave a final sign that looked like a stern dismissal, and a shout of "No."

Ignoring him, and watching her, the dog shook, then lolled its tongue happily. She had to admit he'd gotten the better of the guy.

"Sorry," the blond said, extending his hand to help her up. "He likes people. Especially females. I'm trying to train him, but he's still a puppy and has a short attention span. Are you okay?"

"Fine," she said, smacking the dirt from her t-shirt and jeans as she stood. "Your 'puppy' must weight a hundred pounds. He doesn't run through the vines like that, does he?"

"Nope. He prefers water. And since he's monster-size . . ."

The dog had not moved and Cady feared looking at him would constitute an invitation. "Kraken. Got it," she said.

"Penn," the girl said. "Don't be rude. Introduce us."

Without her hand covering the lower half of her face, Cady saw a striking girl about her own age, with pretty blue eyes. . . . *Penn, did she say Penn? This was the guy from North Carolina who outbid her family for the coveted vines?*

He sent the girl a look of smiling patience. "I'm Penn Abbott, and this is Siobhan Abbott."

Cady drew on the manners instilled by her parents and smiled at the couple who had swooped in and made themselves her new neighbors. "Cady St. Simon."

Siobhan clapped. "Yea! Someone our age. It's been so serious and busy since we got here. Finally, a friend. What's the shopping like? Clothes, I mean.

And restaurants? Any that are associated or connected to wineries?"

"Siobhan. Let her breathe," the man said.

"Oh, sorry," the woman responded, although she didn't look sorry. "Maybe we can have lunch together later this week."

Surprised, but charmed at the woman's enthusiasm and without a ready excuse, Cady blinked and nodded. "Um, sure. Just walk on over. If I'm not in the tasting room, I'm more than likely in the lab. It's the small building next to the winery."

Penn Abbott raised an eyebrow. "*You* work in the lab?"

"Primary enologist for Vines to Water Winery," Cady said, not bothering to hide the irritation in her voice. "And a female, too."

"Oh, he noticed you're a female," Siobhan said, grinning.

Cady frowned. *Was he some kind of player?* Then what was their relationship?

"Wait," Penn said, ignoring the girl by his side and the dog straining at his collar. "You aren't the St. Simon who came up with the Cab rated 94 in last year's *Wine Spectator*?"

Cady crossed her arms. "One and the same."

Siobhan's grin widened as she rubbed her hands together and faced Penn. "Major competition right next door. Smart, pretty, and stands up for herself. I like her."

The word competition caught Cady's attention. The former owners of Silver Vines raised and sold their exquisite grapes to other winemakers. They didn't have a lab or winery to process their grapes or produce their own label, but there was a flat parcel about three acres in size the former owner had left unplanted and had intended to build on. His failing health had forced the subsequent sale of the vineyard.

Her heart sank. "Competition? So, you'll be creating your own label?"

Penn Abbott was easy to read. He didn't appreciate Siobhan blurting out their business plans. It wasn't a mean look though, more of a 'put a cork in it.'

"That's enough, Siobhan."

The wattage in the girl's smile dimmed. "It's a small community, Penn. When you start building and buying equipment, everyone will know you want to put out a label."

An imploring whine drew their attention to Kraken. The big dog shook with wanting to be set free from his master's command.

"Poor fur baby," Cady said, still not glancing at the giant furball. "He wants to play."

"He only obeys a couple of signs so far," Penn said, getting down on one knee in front of the dog. "I'll let him knock me down while the two of you escape."

"Signs?" Cady asked.

"Yes. He was born deaf and we've been teaching him behavior signs."

The blond twisted his wrist and opened his palm close to the dog's face. Kraken quivered even harder. Then pounced.

****

Bracing himself was pitifully inadequate. Kraken's puppy love bites left bruises and sometimes broke the skin. In this kind of free-for-all, his big dirty paws were unavoidable. Penn wrestled with the dog as his sister and Cady St. Simon got away.

After he let the dog maul him for a few minutes, Penn grabbed its muzzle and held it still. "You can't hear me, you monster, but as long as I'm in the dirt, it's time to enforce one of your lessons." He made the sign for the dog to sit and he actually did, although for a short time. Penn hugged him, then stood and dug in his pocket for a treat.

While the dog sat and crunched, Penn glanced at the row of vines Cady St. Simon had walked down. His sister's assessment had been spot-on. Not that he'd let her know that. Even with Kraken's paw prints and smudges of dirt on her face, the pretty redheaded neighbor stirred a longing in him. Too bad he couldn't afford to be side-tracked from his goal.

Penn refocused on his dog and laughed. The shaggy mutt stared longingly at the same space he had. The vines where Cady St. Simon had walked. "Not a chance, buddy. Don't even go there. She's the competition."

Kraken barked, making Penn laugh.

He dusted himself off and headed toward the house, Kraken in tow. Walking the vines calmed him and let him think out his plans for his new property purchase. First, he'd agreed to keep on Rich Morrison, the vineyard manager, instinctively trusting the man who had worked for the former owners for twenty-plus years. Rich and his wife JoAnn had lived in the area all their lives and she volunteered at the local AVA. JoAnn had introduced him and made sure he knew about the calendar of winery events.

The second thing he'd done, almost as soon as he'd unpacked, was hire a local architect to design a top-notch lab and winery. Siobhan was right. Although he had a list of winemakers who wanted to buy his crop, the local wine community would soon find out he meant to use at least some of the extraordinary grapes at Silver Vines to produce his own label.

The house at Silver Vines sat near the road. On his initial visit, he'd been surprised at the stately, Italianate design. It seemed out-of-place in this smallish wine community of southeastern Washington State. Nevertheless, it was comfortable and spacious to the point that his quarters gave him plenty of privacy.

He detoured through his office and put Kraken in his crate, then walked into the large kitchen. Italian design had prevailed here, too. The walls were stucco with a terracotta-colored stain and the floor had tumbled limestone tiles. Siobhan stood adding ingredients to a large saucepan on the commercial-grade range.

She turned to him. "Hey. If it isn't the smooth talker. 'What? That was *you* who made that fine wine?' and 'Duh, I stay here and take on vicious dog while you girls run away.' "

Penn shot her a look. "Exaggerations. Besides, would you rather have yourself or our new neighbor thrown to the ground and slobbered over?"

Siobhan grinned. "She already was. Besides, Kraken stops charging for me. Just sayin', you didn't come off like a keeper."

Penn rolled his gaze up. "Don't know why you insist on putting me in that box. I'm not looking."

She pushed out her bottom lip. "Which is why it's fun to put you there. By the way, that woman from the AVA Alliance called. She said you wanted a referral from them about hiring an enologist with experience as an assistant. Wouldn't you have to have a primary enologist before you need an assistant?"

Penn dropped his head. "She was supposed to call on my cellphone, not the number of the winery.

And I didn't ask for an assistant. I asked for an enologist to assist me in creating a cabernet and some blends."

His sister stirred the contents of her large pan. "The whole upset with the family and the decision to stake a claim where the Abbott name isn't legendary in the wine business means a lot, but putting out your own top-rated label within three years is huge. Your viticulture knowledge is solid, but not so much enology. Up until now . . ."

Penn rubbed two fingers across his forehead. ". . . up until now I've been the front guy. The ring master of the Abbott circus." He pounded the countertop softly with the side of his fist. "Not just a first label, Siobhan. A winning bottle."

"Then I'll do what I can to help," she said.

The side of Penn's mouth lifted. His sister had been thinking about opening her own small restaurant, but had dropped the idea and thrown in with him when the family drama had unfolded. "We'll make it a two-pronged attack. A winning bottle for me and a high-class bistro attached to Silver Vines with you as its chef."

A smile bloomed on Siobhan's face. "Done. I'll donate toward the project. And don't forget to add the kitchen and bistro space to the architect's plans. I'll need to approve, of course."

He peeked into the pan. "I will. Now, what's with the huge amount of clam sauce? There are only two of us, and after only a half a month, the freezer is already full of leftovers."

Siobhan tapped the wood spoon on the side of the pan and didn't meet his gaze. "That's fair. Although I asked Morrison to meet us for lunch so the two of you can discuss vineyard stuff. He can help eat this. I want to see how adding capers and another secret ingredient affects the flavor."

Penn couldn't berate his twin too much. She was a phenomenal chef and one more guinea pig couldn't hurt. "Sounds good."

He walked into his office where Kraken snored in his big crate. A friend back home had mentioned puppies with a golden retriever, and possible Great Pyrenees heritage. Penn had liked Kraken's personality and only found out later that he was born deaf and mostly Great Pyrenees. The crazy dog could drop and sleep anywhere since his world was completely silent.

Penn took the phone from its cradle, intent on returning the call to the AVA Alliance member. His gaze strayed to the office window and the view of his neighbor's property. He smiled, remembering Cady's indignant frown when he expressed surprise at her ownership of the beautiful Cabernet from the previous year. His mistake had been in not mentioning it had been based on the male-dominated wine community he'd grown up in. And her age. Someone being in what he assumed was still in her twenties creating that cab, was amazing. He lifted a shoulder. No guarantee she'd buy *that*.

The number he called answered immediately. "Hello."

"This is Penn Abbott returning your call."

A cheerful voice responded. "Hi, Penn. This is Carole Winston. I've looked into your request and found a couple of suitable and interested candidates."

He relaxed and smiled. With the growing season just beginning, he'd been afraid they wouldn't find anyone with the required credentials. And he wanted first dibs. He grabbed a pencil and pad. "That's great. I can contact them today. Names and numbers?"

"Drew Ford. He's at 509-555-4561. Then, Mason Pritchard at 509-555-2637. Drew has the most experience and has worked as a consultant with a number of local winemakers. Mason is newer to lab work, but he's got an amazing grasp of the history of blends in the area and an enology degree."

"Sounds like I need to make a tough decision," Penn said."

"Good luck. And again, welcome to the AVA."

"Thanks, Carole."

A knock sounded and Rich Morrison poked his head around the doorframe. "Got a minute?"

Penn nodded. "Glad you're early for lunch. Want to run a couple things by you."

The tall, rangy man with salt and pepper hair stepped into the room. He patted his stomach. "Your sister is an amazing cook. My wife is beginning to think I don't like her dinners anymore."

"One of the hazards of new management," Penn said, smiling. "Free use of that giant pool out back, if you want to burn off more calories. Had to put in a new filter system for Kraken. He has an appointment to get a summer haircut, but not for a couple of days."

Rich Morrison smiled back. "So, we'll get to see how big he really is."

"From the size of his feet, my money's on really big. What can I do for you?"

"Vines are in good shape and the UFW crew we hired has approved this year's contract."

"Good news," Penn said. "I could also use your input on some local industry talent."

Morrison rubbed his chin. A sign he was interested in the subject, Penn was learning. "What kind of talent? Vineyard work?"

"No. I'm looking for an enologist with some solid creds to help me work on our first cabernet label. The AVA Alliance has suggested two names. I plan to interview them soon, if they're available. One is a Drew Ford. The other is Mason Pritchard."

An expression Penn had never seen, one of indecision, crossed his vineyard manager's face.

Chapter Two

"Those names bother you?"

Morrison shrugged. "This is a small community. Rumors, politics, infighting, jealousies. You're in the business, so you get it."

Penn nodded. "I do. And you know how serious my goal is to get out a winning label. I need you to be straight with me."

The vineyard manager swung his gaze to Penn. "Thing is, there's nothing substantiated. Just talk and I don't want to color your opinion."

He wanted to hear it anyway. The stakes were too high. "About?"

"About a few local wineries taking on a guy who later made claims about his part in producing their best labels."

"And one of them was a name I mentioned?"

Morrison nodded. "I'd prefer to tell you about credentials instead of rumor."

The man was fair. Something Penn appreciated. "All right. Drew Ford."

"Self-made rather than going the college viti-culture or enology certificate or degree route. Fancies himself a top consultant and can back it up with real world experience, mostly. He's been employed at several wineries in the area."

Penn seized on the word *mostly*. "Mason Pritchard?"

"Highly educated and ambitious. Grandson of one of the valley's original holdings and oldest labels. Out to prove himself, but only has a little hands-on experience under his belt."

Penn's heart sank. An unemployed prima-donna spelled personality clash or sour reputation. On the other hand, two relative newbies feeling their way around a lab didn't equal a great outcome. Maybe the time to prove himself hadn't arrived.

Not willing to give up, Penn shifted a shoulder and tipped his head at his vineyard manager. "Appreciate the information."

****

Cady raised a hand to wave to her dad walking the vines with their manager, but they were deep in conversation and didn't see her. She knew she'd get a rundown at lunch so continued past the house and went into her small, worn-around-the-edges lab. The news she'd learned from the Abbotts unsettled her. She'd heard rumors just yesterday about an upscale winery and lab being designed for Silver Vines and put into production as soon as possible. Siobhan's admission that Penn Abbott wanted to produce his own label made it reality.

Having talked herself out of working, restless energy propelled Cady into the house and her mother's small office, which was really a corner of the kitchen.

"What happened to you?" Helen St. Simon asked, peering over her glasses at Cady.

Cady looked at her paw-printed t-shirt and smiled. "New neighbor's dog got over-friendly."

"I've seen them settling in and been meaning to take over a cake or something. Maybe I should call first or risk ending up on my backside."

Cady saw Desi from the corner of her eye. The black and red-coated miniature pinscher made a beeline for her and sniffed her shoes and pant legs thoroughly. "It's okay Des," she said. "New dog in town named Kraken. He's ten times bigger than you, but he seems friendly. Bonus, he likes females."

"Kraken? As in the sea monster?" her mother asked.

Cady nodded. "Very apt. Hey, did you know the new guy's planning on producing his own label? As soon as possible?"

"I did," came Cord St. Simon's voice from the hall entrance. "He's a very ambitious young man. Can't help himself, I guess."

Cady frowned. "What does that mean?"

Her father smiled. "Too much time in the lab, not enough keeping yourself up-to-date on industry gossip. The Abbotts are wine royalty on the east coast. Their holdings in North Carolina are famous. Their tasting room and most of their bottles are located in a privately-owned cavern on their estate."

She put fisted hands on her hips. Great. It wasn't enough that he was good-looking and obviously moneyed. He also came from wine royalty. "Of course I've heard the name, but it's fairly common so I didn't make the connection. So, what are two members of this famous winemaking clan doing clear across the country?"

Cord St. Simon shook his head. "Family blowup. Sad really. Father married a local widow after his wife passed away and within a year, the twins were all but cut out of the business."

"What twins?" Cady and her mother chorused.

Her father sighed. "I thought women were supposed to be up on all the gossip. Penn and his sister, Siobhan, are fraternal twins. Oh, and Honey, Siobhan is considered a multi-star chef, so that better be a good cake." He turned and whistled his way down the hall.

"Guess he told us," Cady's mother said. "But hey, a handsome single guy interested in wine. And right next door."

"I heard competition, Mom. That's what I heard. And how do you know he's handsome?"

Helen St. Simon pushed her glasses back upon her nose and sniffed. "I get out. Saw him yesterday when I drove to the grocery store. He waved."

"Well don't start picking out wedding invitation card stock. As I said, he's the competition."

Her mother slumped. "Desi's pitter patter of little feet is all I'm getting is what you're telling me."

"For now, Mom. For now."

Contrary to her words, warmth pooled in Cady's stomach at the mention of Penn Abbott's single status. Didn't guarantee he didn't have a girlfriend in North Carolina or a fiancée who would be joining him here. Not that she cared.

Cady shook off the musing. More prize-winning cabernets to prove last year's wasn't a fluke, had to be her top priority. And she wouldn't be distracted by a nice, new man who wanted to save her from his dog.

"I'll make it simple," her mother said, already moving on. "A mandarin orange cake with a brown sugar glaze." She pushed up her glasses and went back to her paperwork. "You can deliver it."

Cady laughed out loud. "You just keep on trying, Mom."

Her mother huffed a breath. "I'm *trying* to finish these invoices. Will you heat up the chicken casserole sitting on the counter and put those slices of Texas Toast in, too? We'll eat in a half hour."

****

At lunch, Cady fidgeted and pushed her food around until her dad tapped the table to get her attention. "Something bothering you?"

She punched the air with her fork. "What I don't get is, what's the hurry? If everything we've heard is true, why does he want to put out a label so soon? Takes most newbies years to get out a bottle of the caliber he's talking about."

"Um, the competition?" her dad said.

"Yeah, he's the competition. I get that."

He grinned. "Now you're just embarrassing yourself."

"You've lost me."

Cord St. Simon put down his fork and folded his hands. "Abbott Estates is hosting a national competition called the Abbott Challenge in three years to celebrate their 75th anniversary and introduce the best new cabs in the country."

"Oooh. Got it. Our new neighbor is trying to prove himself. Bummer." Cady shook her head. "Even with premium grapes and the best lab in town, he'll need a premium enologist on top of it and a ton of luck."

Her dad held her gaze. "He's considering Drew."

Cady's fork clattered to the table. "How did you . . . when did you . . .?"

"Just before lunch. As a member of the Alliance, they passed the information about the candidates Mr. Abbott was looking for, to me. Drew and one other."

Helen St. Simon interrupted. "How can they possibly recommend him as a viable candidate after what he's pulled?"

"He said, she said, Mom," Cady put in. "He made sure there were enough people on his side to make the claim. He lost, true, but we all know he still feeds the rumors." She took a deep breath, "excuse me," and escaped to her lab. The place she was rarely interrupted. Except when, in her zeal to improve a blend, she forgot to eat or sleep. Her parents would step in and treat her like a twelve-year-old and make her come in.

As she worked, her thoughts drifted to the Abbotts. She'd developed an excellent cabernet with decent grapes and a lot of hard work. Could Penn, with his limited lab experience, develop a prize-winning formula with the premium grapes at Silver Vines? Grapes, yes. But Cady believed in her heart that it took a masterful touch and lots of lab time. And hoped against hope Penn wouldn't hire Drew.

****

Lunch over, Penn went back to his office and pulled up his email. His architect had sent a preliminary, simplified design of his new lab. She was still working on drawings of the winery. He opened the design and smiled.

"What are you grinning at?" Siobhan asked as she walked to peer over his shoulder. "Good grief. It looks like parts of a gourmet kitchen. Heating, cooling, prep islands, storage for glassware and tools." She pointed to an area near the proposed tasting room. "This would be perfect for a kitchen and seating for my bistro. Visitors could stop in the tasting room then walk down a short hallway to the restaurant. When will they start building?"

"Not for a couple of weeks. She still has to get the permits and find a contractor. That'll be rough. All the top crews are already booked through the year."

"You're cutting it close," Siobhan said. "If worst comes to worst, could you rent space in another lab, like commercial kitchens rent to small catering firms? You're going to need a winery to process, too."

"Penn shrugged. "Hadn't thought of that as an option. But I'll check into it. Thanks for the suggestion."

"Sure. What did that woman at the alliance have to say?"

He huffed a breath, "She gave me two names. Possible assistants."

"That sounds like good news. Why the sigh?"

"I asked Morrison for his take. He didn't say anything overly negative, said he wanted me to form my own impressions but I got the sense one of them was a prima-donna with a poor reputation for staying at any one place. Which could be interpreted as he was asked to leave. The other's enthusiasm is his best asset, but it doesn't make up for his lack of skill."

"Maybe it's not your time to win."

"My thought, too," Penn said. "But if wanting to win counts, I have to try." That was it in a nutshell. This was a huge undertaking and he questioned his decision almost daily. The answer was always the same. He still wanted it.

Siobhan leaned to hug him. "Your choice isn't going to change how people feel about you."

"Yeah."

"Then, good luck with your interviews."

He nodded and pulled out his cellphone as Siobhan left. "Better make some calls."

Mason Pritchard answered on the first ring. "S'up?"

"Um, this is Penn Abbott. I'm looking for Mason Pritchard."

"Oh, hi. This is Mason. Sorry for the casual greeting. I belong to a Facebook group that's planning a flash mob at a winery event. I didn't recognize the number."

"Different plan," said Penn. "The AVA alliance gave me your contact information. I'm setting up a lab and winery at Silver Vines and looking for an enologist. They said you might be interested."

"Wait. Did you say Abbott? As in Abbott Estates?"

Can't get away from the name, even clear across the country. "Another branch of the family tree."

"Oh. I mean yes. I'm interested. Very interested."

"Are you available for an interview?" Penn asked. If enthusiasm counted, Mason qualified.

"Any time."

"How about tomorrow morning at 9:00?"

"You got it. And thanks, Mr. Abbott."

Penn hung up. *Young.* But the viticulture and enology degrees and family history were bonuses. Maybe they could learn the practical, together.

He stood and went through the French doors to the expansive patio. This view took in another angle of the Vines to Water Winery, where the very talented Cady St. Simon lived and worked. At least he figured she lived there. And was lab talent so much on his mind it superseded his thoughts of a very pretty redhead?

Maybe Siobhan could . . .? He shook his head. Can't go there. Siobhan would take his request to learn more about Cady as a sign she should become a matchmaker. Safer to step cautiously by himself. His head jerked as an idea came to him. Cady St. Simon would be a great lab partner. Partner more than in the lab? *Whoa.* Bad idea. Neighbors and competitors didn't make for good partners. Of any kind.

Penn logged onto the internet. He spent a half hour trying his luck on websites, then leaned back in his chair. "Well that was fruitless," he said out loud.

"What was?" his sister asked coming through the door.

"Checked around to see if there was lab and winery space available for rent. No success."

He straightened and tapped the desktop. "Here's an idea. Why don't we throw a 'get to know us' open house? You can be the chef and plan the menu and I'll be the front man, as usual. Only this time, I'm not pushing Abbott Estates' line of wines, I'm looking for possible lab space, local contractors, and eno-logist referrals."

"I like it," Siobhan said.

Penn grinned. "Won't hurt to get a few more names in case neither one I have works out."

"Your desperation is showing again," she said, starting to turn. "I'll go plan the menu for our first event at Silver Vines."

****

Cady paced her lab. She couldn't turn off the image looping in her head of Penn hiring Drew and having him next door. It had been over half a year and she'd managed to avoid situations where he'd likely attend. She'd even refused to stay at a function when she saw his car in the parking lot.

The anger at his deception in the lab had dissipated, as had the hurt regarding their personal relationship. She sighed. Apparently, Drew intended on staying in the valley and working in the wine industry. She couldn't help that. And she wouldn't go running over to Silver Vines telling tales about her former lab assistant.

Cady's thoughts were interrupted by a soft knock at the door. Since her trust had been broken by Drew, she locked the lab when she remembered. For sure when she wasn't inside. She called out, "Coming."

Siobhan Abbott stood outside. "Hi. Is it too soon to visit? I mean are you really busy?"

Cady smiled. She had liked her new neighbor immediately. "Not at all. Come in. I'd appreciate the company."

Siobhan stepped in and looked around. "This is nice."

"Although much smaller than the lab or labs, I should think, at Abbott Estates," Cady said.

"I paid no attention. My world has always been centered in the kitchen."

Cady nodded. "Dad said you were a pretty spectacular chef. It appears you and I like to create."

The brunette lifted a shoulder. "That's a good way of putting it. I came to ask you two things. I know this sounds pushy, since we only met a few hours ago, but I think lunch is a great idea. At a winery with a restaurant, please. I'd value your recommendation since we've decided to add a small bistro with me as its chef."

Cady clapped. "That's a great idea. Everyone who comes out to try your tasting room and bistro may decide to wander over to our tasting room, and vice versa. What was the second thing?"

"Since we're neighbors, I wanted you to know Penn and I are planning an open house. Kind of an 'under new management,' thing. We'll send out invitations of course, but I wanted to invite you personally." Siobhan grinned. "And I thought if we went to lunch, I could pump you for some names you think would be appropriate. People we should get to know. Would that be okay?"

Direct and polite, Cady thought. No guile that she could discern. They'd only been here a short time and the girl was probably lonely having grown up clear across the country. There also must be a strong bond with her brother for her to have left everything to come here and start over. "'Course it would," Cady said. "How about if I pick you up at 11:30 day after tomorrow? I'll put together a list we can go over during lunch."

Siobhan came to her toes for an instant. "Love that plan, thanks." She hesitated. "Would you mind trading cellphone numbers? I know some people don't like to give theirs out."

"Not at all," Cady rattled off her number when Siobhan pulled out her phone.

Siobhan held up her phone. "Looking forward to hearing from you."

Cady gave a finger wave as her new friend left. It'd be nice to have another woman to hang out with. Her good friend Adrienne had gotten married last year. Swept off her feet by a young winemaker from California who was attending a seminar hosted by a local AVA. Cady sighed. She and Adrienne Skyped and talked on the phone, but not as often as she liked.

She smiled to herself. Being close to the sister of Penn Abbott couldn't hurt either. *Not so fast trusting the handsome blond.* She'd made that mistake with Drew Ford.

Cady retied her apron and went back to work.

As if thinking about Penn Abbott made him appear, Cady heard a hard bump against her door. Um, wouldn't he knock?

She undid the lock, opened it, and Kraken nearly bowled her over, his paws planted on her shoulders, a happy face greeting her. She made sure he could see her hand, then imitated the shooing motion Penn had used on him this morning. To her delight, he dropped and sat.

"Fast learner," came Penn Abbott's tenor.

Cady jerked toward the door, but Kraken just lolled his tongue and squirmed.

"He seems to have invited himself," she said, brushing her hands down her apron. "Or maybe he smells Desi."

"Desi?"

"My miniature pinscher," Cady said.

"Suits you," Penn replied.

She laughed. "She also considers this lab her territory. There'll be bobbing eyebrows and thorough sniffing to suss out the invader."

"I'm curious. Is her name short for Desdemona? Very Shakespearean."

"Ducati Desmo," Cady responded. "Italian motorcycle that used to be a bad habit of mine."

Penn's mouth opened, then closed without any sound coming out.

Cady shrugged. "As I said, 'used to be.' "

"Expensive," Penn commented.

"Not really. It belonged to my uncle. He bought it second-hand before he deployed overseas. It had been well taken care of. He's back and it's gone."

She really enjoyed the look, of what? Bafflement? Envy? Most definitely, surprise.

He had been leaning against the doorjamb, but pushed away. "Light traffic on 82. Did you get to open it up?"

She nodded. "The Italians know their speed machines. It was a sweet ride."

Cady noticed Kraken's squirming had increased and he had edged closer.

Penn noticed, too. "I took him for a walk and he made a beeline for your lab. I'm really sorry. We've considered installing one of those invisible fences, but are going to try an ergonomic leash first. I plan to get one in the next few days." He paused. "If you had my cell number, you could call me the next time he gets away and bothers you. If I don't catch him."

Cady pulled her cellphone out of her back pocket. "Ready."

He gave her his number. "Mind if I have yours? Just so we're covered."

Pretty smooth she thought. "Shouldn't be an issue if you use that leash, but good to know my helpful new neighbor has my back." What had possessed her to say that? It sounded like flirting.

Penn winked. "Neighbor-helping-neighbor."

"Sure," Cady said, not curbing her eye roll, but giving her number. "Love your dog, but if he gets carried away, and bumps a workbench with glassware . . ."

"Oh, right," Penn stepped in to take Kraken by the collar. He bent and turned the dog's face to his. "Not today, boy. Or we won't be invited back."

Cady was tempted to point out that they weren't invited in the first place, but decided not to. Mostly because she liked the dog *and* his master and wanted to stay on friendly terms. She also wanted desperately to warn Penn about Drew. That was neighbor-helping-neighbor, right? Cady shook her head. Nope. She wouldn't stoop to Drew's level.

Penn threw a full wattage smile her way as he half carried Kraken out the door, the dog whining in protest.

She released a slow breath. A girl could do worse. A lot worse.

Chapter Three

An intriguing girl, Penn thought, as he and his unwilling dog headed back to Silver Vines. And he figured he'd only scratched the surface. Top notch enologist, dog lover, pretty without pushing it, and a few minutes ago, learning she liked driving the edge. What else didn't he know about Cady St. Simon? The biggest question being was there a boyfriend or special someone in her life? He hoped not.

Kraken dragged him to a stop, thankfully doing his doggie business on their property. Afterward, Penn held the dog's face steady and repeated a sign until he could see it was understood. "Time for you to take a nap in your crate, buddy. That way we'll all have some peace."

Kraken headed straight for Penn's office.

Penn went into the kitchen to find Siobhan, head down, concentrating on her laptop.

"Something interesting?"

She didn't look up. "Menu for the party. Cady's going to help."

Apparently, the pretty redhead hadn't ducked fast enough, but she would learn. He waited.

Siobhan paused. "We're going to lunch. She's bringing me an 'A' list of people we should know in the valley. And those who should know us."

"Handy," Penn said.

"Yup. She's nice that way. And it gives me a chance to tell people my name is pronounced Sha Vahn. Not Cee O Bon."

Good for her. She took a lot of grief over her unusual name. As far as her assessment of Cady, his sister's intuition rang true almost one hundred percent. Another tick mark in Cady's favor. She was garnering a lot of them in a short time.

Penn leaned against Siobhan's desk. "Speaking of lists. I need to put some questions together for the interviews I'm conducting. Any suggestions?"

She looked up. "Probably the tangibles, like job history and education, and intangibles, like do you think you're reliable, punctual, easy to work with, take direction well, stuff like that. Make sure to tell them what's important to you."

Penn pulled his lips in then out. "Good points, but I'm uneasy about there being only two choices so far. If I expanded my search to nearby AVAs, I'd have another pool of prospects. Think I'll go online for some sample job interview questions and maybe pick Rich's brain. Call me for dinner?"

Siobhan nodded, her focus back on her party menu.

****

His question about punctuality was answered the next day at 8:55 a.m. when Mason Pritchard knocked on the door. He looked even younger than Penn's perception during their phone conversation. Mason was tall and thin with a full-mouth smile and a firm handshake.

Penn had Googled Prichard Cellars in advance of the meeting and learned they were a well-respected mid-sized winery that used primarily their own grapes as the basis for their wines. Something he was interested in doing.

Penn lead Mason into his office, noticing he held no paperwork. "Did you bring a resume?"

"Looked up your email and sent it to you a couple of hours ago." Mason tipped his head. "Not much of interest on it. My viticulture and enology degrees are really new. I also have a minor in chemistry. My actual lab experience is limited. I basically worked every job at Pritchard Cellars. Drudge work in the vineyard, tuning the ATVs we use, rotating the barrels, designing event flyers." He grinned. "And manning the tasting room after I turned twenty-one, about a year ago."

A digital resume hadn't occurred to him, so Penn walked to his desk, flipped open his laptop, then pointed to a nearby chair.

Sure enough, the resume was the second item in his inbox. "Give me a minute to read this."

Mason nodded and looked around.

Reading the resume didn't take long as it appeared straightforward. Penn set aside his stock questions for a minute and went with curiosity. "How come you want to work for somebody else since your whole family seems to be in the business?"

The guy squirmed a little. "Three generations makes for a sizeable number of Pritchards. Everyone is entrenched in a niche. Our lab is run by my uncle, and his two sons, my cousins, are his assistants. I'd like to have my own winery one day and decided early on that creating great wines was the way to do it." He shrugged. "Besides, Silver Vines grapes are amazing. You can hardly go wrong."

Penn appreciated his directness, and admired somebody who had the same idea about making it on his own. He felt he had to be upfront about his requirements. "My experience in the lab is almost nil. Tell me how you think the two of us are going to produce an award-winning label to roll out in three years."

Mason swallowed visibly and blinked. "When?"

Penn repeated himself.

"Um, will there be anyone helping us who has real experience?"

He didn't blame Mason for the question. Even with the incredible grapes at their disposal, it would be difficult. Had he bitten off too much? Would his father even care if Penn entered and received high praise for a cab he'd produced on his own?

Put that way, Penn didn't think so. His stepmother ran things from day one and influenced his father's views. On the other hand, a highly-rated bottle would bring tremendous self-satisfaction.

He shook his head, answering Mason's question and bringing on a frown. Penn allowed himself a sigh. He had hoped for more enthusiasm. A "Let's give them a run for it." Judging from the look on Mason's face, he might have already lost him.

The rest of the interview proved average, and Penn thought they were both happy to have it over. He shook hands and told Mason he'd be making a decision soon.

Penn walked back into the kitchen. Siobhan turned from her desk and raised an eyebrow. "That much fun?"

"Nice guy, but a little short on eagerness. I think he pictured a learning or training situation over a number of years."

"He didn't realize you were already in a race," she said. "I know you have another shot at someone who has experience, but if I send out the invitations in the form of an e-vite, we can have our event by middle of next week since weekends are busiest time for wineries. You can fish for names and possible referrals."

"That could work. And thanks for running with this and pulling it together. You have the expertise for the menu. What say we use the great room, and if the nice spring weather holds, overflow onto the patio?"

Siobhan held up a piece of paper. "Here's the first draft of the menu. Hot Tapas and uncomplicated hors d'oeuvres. Throw in some bite-sized sweets and that should do it. I'm depending on Cady's kindness and knowledge to recommend some local wines to go with. You know, serve wines produced by our guests. I'll let you know how many guests as soon as I sort out the list she's helping with. Anyone you want to invite?"

He grinned. "Everyone in the St. Simon household."

"That's a given. So are Rich and JoAnn. What about your two interviewees?"

"Guess it'd be rude not to. Speaking of which, I need to call the other guy and get him scheduled."

Back in his office, Penn walked to the desk to refer to his notes and pulled out his cellphone. As with the call to Mason, it was answered on the first ring.

"Thought you'd get around to me."

Penn looked at the piece of paper in his hand with the numbers on it. "Excuse me?"

A chuckle sounded on the other end. "You have the right person. This is Drew Ford. News travels fast in the wine community. You talked to Mason this morning, and now you want to talk to me. The best for last."

Marketing was Penn's comfort zone, so he knew a salesman when he heard one. He tried not to judge, because over confidence wasn't always a bad thing. Some people used it to cover nerves. "Do you know my availability for that interview?"

Crickets sounded. Then, "I hope soon. I have another offer pending."

Penn smiled. Easy enough to check. He could play this game all day. "Oh. Am I too late? I wouldn't want to waste your time. Who made the other offer?"

"Afraid I'm not at liberty to say."

Big shock there. "Can you make it 8:30 tomorrow morning? And a brief resume if you have one."

"You mind if we make it 9:00? Got a hot date tonight and I may want to sleep in. Know what I mean?"

Penn considered canceling the interview altogether. This guy obviously thought he was the only egg in the basket and was pushing it, but Penn had checked it out and knew better. There were several more AVAs in southeastern Washington, and he didn't want to pay someone's moving expenses, but to get a good enologist from another area in here, he would.

"Not getting off to a good start, but sure. See you at 9:00."

Penn pushed out a breath. Was it worth making bad compromises because he desperately needed a good enologist?

Drew Ford had better have some sterling experience.

****

Cord St. Simon approached Cady, his head tilted in a questioning angle. "How come you're walking in the vines this morning instead of holing up in the lab?"

Cady stretched the truth. She didn't want her dad to know how much Drew's interview and possible hire-on at Silver Vines bothered her. She hadn't slept well the night before, but smiled. "Too nice to stay inside, so, I'm on my way to the beach. Wanted to put in some thinking time about the blends I'm going to work on this year."

Her dad laughed. "Just because the vineyard runs to the edge of the river, then drops to the water, doesn't mean there's a real beach. But you keep believing that."

Cady twisted her lips wryly. "Hey it's right next to the water so, technically, it's a beach."

She'd been twelve when her parents bought the lot that slanted down to the river, determined to grow several varietals of wine grapes and eventually open a winery. After the business was up and running, she'd tried hard, and got them to name it Vines to Water.

"You haven't answered my question," her father said.

Cady tried for nonchalance. "Poor sleep last night, really. Too many formulas dancing in my head.

If you could use an extra hand in the vines this morning, though. I'm your girl."

Her father didn't speak for a moment. Just looked at her. He could usually ease her distress, but this wasn't frustration over a botched blend. He shrugged. "Abbott sounds like a reasonable man. Happy to have a chat with him about Ford. He might be grateful."

She hadn't thought of it that way. Penn was so new to the area, he wouldn't know Drew's history. Cady tilted her head and wondered for the hundredth time why the jerk had stayed in the area after maligning the reputations of three labs.

Because he's told enough lies to get away with it.

For a long time, she'd felt like a victim. So enamored by her good-looking, sweet-talking help, Cady had put the rumors down to jealousy and ignored them. After the whole mess came to light, she'd stayed close to home and worked solo, swearing to herself that's the way it would stay. She huffed a sigh, then shook her head. "Thanks, Dad, but Penn's a big boy and will figure it out."

A car's engine drew their attention as a green Subaru crested the rise in the road between the two vineyards and turned west to Silver Vines. But not before its headlights flicked on and off in greeting. "Ass," Cady murmured and lifted a shoulder. "Back to the lab for all lab rats."

"Catch you at lunch," her dad said.

"Nope. Lunch with my new friend, Siobhan. Catch you later."

She cast a glance at the driveway to the house at Silver Vines. "Be careful Penn Abbott."

Her mood lifted as she headed for the house. She hadn't realized how much she needed this mini break, until . . . Cripes. The list she'd promised Siobhan was only half done. A peek at her phone showed a little past nine. If she concentrated, it could be finished in a half hour. Then, plenty of time to get ready.

Chapter Four

C ady leaned forward and stretched her neck as she rounded the curve in the driveway to Silver Vines. She relaxed. No green Subaru, and no chance of running into Drew. Hopefully that meant he and Penn hadn't hit it off.

She approached the hand-carved door with stylized grape-cluster knocker and vines for door handles. They were made of copper-clad cast iron and very dramatic. She raised her hand to knock when Penn opened the door.

Damn. He got better looking each time she saw him. Today he wore rust-colored long-sleeved shirt rolled to his elbows and very snug jeans. Cady pulled in her lips for an instant and squelched the urge to whistle. She knew from personal experience good looks could hide a nasty personality.

"You look nice," he said smiling, then turned down his mouth comically. "Sadly, you're the reason I have to scrounge for my own lunch today."

Cady smiled back. "Poor you. No one to stand over a hot stove and serve from the left."

"Ouch."

"But right on target," came Siobhan's voice from behind him. "Let's go, Cady. Leave Mr. Pathetic to his scrounging."

They both giggled as they got in her car.

Cady congratulated herself on her choice of clothes. She'd decided to dress a level higher than she usually did when going out to lunch. Siobhan looked chic in a turquoise silk shirt with a square collar, worn over khaki linen slacks.

"So looking forward to today," Siobhan chirped as she put on sleek sunglasses against the bright spring sun. "One more teensy favor? Although I feel like I've already used up my allotment. The internet shows a Costco in Kennewick. Is that close to the winery where we're eating? I need grande´ sizes of some ingredients and foods for our party."

"Sure. Maybe ten or twelve minutes farther. We can stop by after lunch."

She took Siobhan to a winery with nationally-rated attached restaurant as requested, so her new friend could scope out the possible competition. The local cuisine did itself proud. They took advantage of the predominantly Mediterranean menu and split a wood-fired flatbread pizza.

Cady decided to tease Siobhan. "One street over from Costco is a little shopping center with a nice jewelry store, a spa, and a home décor shop that also has cute clothes."

Siobhan squealed. "I see lots of lunches in our future."

"Me, too. You'll need an occasional break from settling in and starting a new business."

"That part is mostly Penn," said Siobhan. "We kept Rich Morrison on, and he seems great. But we need a business manager and people to work in the winery and lab we're adding. I'll be running the bistro."

Cady couldn't help herself. "Has Penn found an enologist he wants to hire?"

Siobhan scrunched her nose. "He got a couple of referrals from the local AVA. The guy he interviewed yesterday was young and had the education, but almost no hands-on. Not much help there." She took another bite of pizza and chewed thoughtfully. "The one he talked to this morning, Drew somebody, has the experience, but neither of us were crazy about his personality. That can be hard to overcome in a day-to-day job environment."

Cady struggled with opening up to Siobhan, but instinctively trusted her. "I've worked with Drew. He's very knowledgeable in the lab. Unfortunately, we had personal and professional differences and parted ways."

Her new friend grinned. "Mind if I ask if the personal differences included his aggressive charm?"

Cady laughed out loud. She'd learned too late about Drew's practice of hitting on any pretty woman he came across. And Siobhan was certainly pretty. "Well put."

"No rush to hire, anyway," Siobhan said. "Penn's working on some other options. Besides, the blueprints still need to be approved by the county and a contractor hired to build it. That'll take some time."

"I might be able to help there. A member of our wine club is a reputable contractor. I can smooth the way, if you're interested. He might be booked, but able to recommend someone else."

Her lunch companion nodded. "Absolutely. I'll have Penn call you."

****

Penn shoved away from his desk and leaned back in his chair. So far he hadn't caught a break in finding an enologist to work with. Maybe he was too picky. Or too late. He'd just crossed the second of three AVAs off his list of possible referrals for hire. "Sorry," they'd said. The winery business was booming and there weren't enough experienced enologists or winery workers as it was, but good luck.

Yeah. Good luck. Reconsidering Drew Ford looked to be a real possibility. The guy's abrasive personality might have to take a back seat to his valuable experience. Penn mentally reviewed the interview. After reading the resume, in which Drew had noted his part in developing several awarded wines and also with an abundance of big words, Penn was impressed and about to say so when Drew said, "I have a contract for you to sign if you offer me the job."

New to vineyard ownership, Penn had had a moment of confusion. "Is that a standard thing here?"

"It is for me," Drew had said.

"Why would you think *you* need a contract and not the other way around?"

The guy had leaned forward conspiratorially and said he had come up with some proprietary blends that other labs had taken advantage of. His contract protected him and made sure he got credit for the blends he'd developed if any dispute came up. A big grin had followed. "Your grapes would be perfect for a high-rated cab right off the bat."

Penn sighed. He hadn't been able to shake the feeling his candidate wasn't telling the complete truth in answer to some questions. At the end, he'd told Drew to shoot him an email with a copy of his contract attached, and that he had other people to see.

"Don't wait too long," had been Drew's response.

Having learned experienced enologists were in demand in the area, Penn had wondered why his interviewee hadn't been snapped up already.

He also hadn't liked the way Drew had ogled Siobhan when she'd introduced herself.

Penn shook his head. Something or someone would come along.

The afternoon sun warmed the back of his neck. He rubbed it and stood. Siobhan kept iced coffee and sweet tea in the refrigerator. A glass of either on the patio would be nice. He glanced at his watch. Siobhan and Cady were gone a long time for a lunch. His sister had been itching to see more of the area. He was sure she'd wangled extra side trips out of Cady.

Halfway through Penn's tea on the patio, Morrison approached from the vines. "Had a chance to interview anyone yet?"

Penn nodded. "Both of them."

His vineyard manager laughed. "You're face tells the story. Maybe next year?"

"Not giving up after two interviews."

"Yoo hoo! Penn."

He shifted an eyebrow toward the front of the house. "Siobhan. No doubt shopping has occurred and she needs help with her haul. I'd like to discuss the results of the interviews with you later. That okay?"

Morrison nodded. "Give me a call."

Penn took another sip of his tea, then remembered Cady might still be there. His afternoon just got brighter. He speed-walked to the driveway where he found Cady surveying the huge amount of groceries in the trunk of her car.

She picked up a giant box of gourmet crackers, a large jar of olives, and a round of cheese. "Siobhan said bring it all into the pantry except the stuff that needs refrigeration." She grinned. "You *do* know where the pantry is?"

"Cute," Penn said, walking toward her. He liked it that she felt comfortable enough to tease him.

The attack came from the far corner of the house and she didn't see it coming. His only chance to stop it was to block the onslaught with his body. Penn took three long strides and dove, hoping he'd hit grass instead of asphalt an instant before he collided with Kraken.

He heard the squeal and saw Cady's quick sidestep as the big dog's jump ended mid-air.

Ten seconds later, Penn opened his eyes and knew Kraken had survived the collision because the dog was licking his face. Cady kneeled beside him and pushed at Kraken. "Penn? Are you okay?"

His former glory days as a tight end on his high school football team had earned him a dislocated shoulder halfway through the season. Laying on the grass beside the driveway brought back that painful memory.

He blinked back tears. "Got the wind knocked out of me."

Kraken appeared delighted that one of his staff lay on the ground to play with. Penn made the sign for crate and the dog drooped his head and walked away.

Siobhan walked up to stand over Penn, hands on hips. "This is not helping."

Cady started laughing and pointed to the articles on the ground. "I started to carry those in, when Kraken came around the corner and charged. Penn threw himself at the dog and both landed here." She shook her head, holding out her hand to help him up. "That was amazing. Wish I'd caught it on video. You're my hero."

Siobhan looked at the big glass jar of olives. "That could have been bad. I owe you an apology."

"Accepted," he said, rubbing his shoulder.

Siobhan directed the placement of the groceries, then they sat at the breakfast bar. "Cady's offered to put us in touch one of her wine club members who's a reputable contractor."

Penn smiled in spite of his throbbing shoulder. "Best news I've had all day,"

Siobhan stood and walked to the large refrigerator, pulled an ice pack from the freezer side and handed it to him. "I told her about your interviews. She's worked with Drew Ford."

It really *was* a small wine community, Penn thought. "Is that right? Maybe you can give me the scoop on him. I can't seem to get anything tangible other than his experience."

Cady's expression stilled. "Actually, he's worked for a number of wineries in the area. I'm sure they're on his resume. My personal experience with him didn't end well, so I'd rather not wade in."

Apparently, Morrison wasn't the only one reticent to talk about Ford. Unless it was a conspiracy, things didn't bode well for the second interviewee's chances at Silver Vines. "Oh, okay. Um, you'll get back to me on that contractor's information?"

Cady backed toward the door, nodding. "I had a great time today, Siobhan. Let me know if you have any questions about the list I gave you."

****

Cady drove across the road, put her car away and headed for her bedroom. Had she made a mistake withholding her opinion of Drew and revealing their history? If she didn't say anything, Penn could get blindsided by Drew's technical skills. And she had no idea what the other vintners he'd worked for would say about him. If she did say something and Drew found out, he would breathe new life into his original rumor that she's lied about his contribution because he didn't respond to the closer relationship she wanted.

Part of her didn't want to admit she'd spent so much alone time in her lab that she'd interpreted all the attention Drew had given her, as love. So stupid. Never mind that he'd showed up late and left early on a regular basis, worked whenever he felt like it, and insisted to everyone who asked, and some who hadn't, that his contribution to the top-rated cab, had been essential.

Would Penn automatically believe 'a guy' over her? Hard to tell, but he hadn't put a foot wrong, so far. He was patient, liked dogs, which was important to her, hardworking, damned good looking, loved by his sister, oh, and brave. Having saved her from a ravenous dog slurping or worse.

Regarding her earlier assessment, made a few days ago, Cady still didn't know if he had a girlfriend or fiancée in North Carolina who could come winging to Washington any day. Now, she was starting to care.

Chapter Five

"You're a million miles away."

Cady turned from folding her favorite silk sweater. "Lots going on."

Her mom smiled. "How'd lunch go? You were gone a long time."

Helen St. Simon spent most of her time contributing to the running of St. Simon Winery. She wouldn't have it any other way, but as a result, she didn't get out a lot. This did not curb her love of gossip, so Cady obliged. "It was great. Warm enough to eat on the restaurant's patio. We shared a wood-fired pizza."

"Yum," her mother said. "Where else did you go?"

"They're throwing a 'get to know us,' event. Siobhan is preparing the food and I helped her with a list of people they might want to invite. It's early in the season, so it's a good time to introduce themselves. Also, she hasn't had time to stock her kitchen with much more than the zillion jars of spices she had shipped here. I took her to Costco to pick up some essentials and stuff for her party. I still owe them a list of local wines to go with, after I see the menu."

Her mom nodded. "Speaking of food, I baked that mandarin orange cake this morning. If there's any chance of getting it over there whole, you should probably take it today."

"Not me," Cady said. "Don't want to wear out my welcome."

Helen St. Simon frowned. "Did they bring up Drew Ford?"

"Yes and no," Cady said. "Penn interviewed him this morning and wanted my opinion. I told him I preferred not to comment."

"Way to avoid trashing someone who desperately needs to be trashed."

"Not going to stir up something that needs to stay unstirred," Cady retorted.

Her mother sighed. "Is there any hope you're attracted to that handsome young man?"

Cady didn't answer right away. She should have been prepared for the question, though, since asking it was one of her mother's favorite hobbies. "Define attracted."

"Cady Leigh St. Simon."

Uh, oh. Middle name. Uncontrolled eye roll. "Of course. He's gorgeous." She didn't add all his other perceived attributes. Not going there.

"Glad you noticed. Okay, I'll take the cake over."

"There's cake?"

Cady and her mother laughed as her dad peered around her door.

"Walking down the hall minding my own business when I distinctly heard the word cake."

"Yes, dear. A welcome cake for our new neighbors."

"I don't suppose you made two?"

Helen St. Simon grinned. "As a matter of fact, I did."

Cady shook her head. "I'll let the two of you work it out. I need to talk to Adrienne."

"Say hello for us," Helen St. Simon said as she joined her husband in the hallway.

"Will do," Cady said, opening her laptop and logging onto Skype. Adrienne worked half days so they made it a habit to chat face-to-face on Tuesdays and if anything interesting came up, on Thursdays, too.

Adrienne's smiling face appeared, her office in the background. "Hi."

"Hey. What's new? Other than I heard this is going to be a terrible wildfire season in your valley."

Adrienne nodded. "Yeah, we heard that, too. The vineyard here has some pretty stiff preventive measures in place, though. Anything new with you?"

Cady waited a beat too long and Adrienne's face came close to the camera. "Spill."

"You know we lost the bid on Silver Vines."

Her friend nodded.

"Well, I met the new owners three days ago."

"And? Don't make me drag it out of you. Are they trolls with terrible breath, or three lonely bachelors who look like Liam Hemsworth?"

"Actually, I think Penn might be a little taller than the Aussie. And Penn is blond."

Adrienne squealed. "What's he like?"

"He's very nice," Cady hedged. "He's single, smart, good-looking, loves dogs, and has a twin sister who adores him."

Adrienne's head was nodding vigorously. "You wouldn't be talking about him unless you liked him. Does he feel the same?"

"All in good time. There's something there on both sides, but it's only been three days. It can hardly be love."

"Don't be ridiculous. Of course it can. Remember when I met Jason? I thought I was only in lust, but in the back of my mind I knew it was something bigger. It's been amazing, Cady. And it *can* be real."

"That's quite a sales pitch."

"Just sayin', you don't want to mess with real. You could lose."

Lose what she hadn't had a chance to know if it was real? Lose Penn? Cady felt her stomach seize up.

"Put that way, I should probably be more open to finding out."

"Yes! And please send me a picture of the two of you together."

****

Penn paced his office. What was going on? What was it about this Ford character that had the last two people he asked for an opinion so reluctant? Actually, Siobhan had told him Cady had said personal *and* professional differences. She hadn't expanded on either and he wondered more about the personal than the professional. Had she and Ford been an item? Not his business as far as the guy's lab skills, but it bothered him more than it should.

He picked up his cellphone and called Morrison. "Got a minute to revisit that discussion about Ford?"

A short pause ensued. "Give me five minutes?"

"Sure. My office."

Penn spent the time going over the resume Ford had given him. Cady was right. There were three other references listed as places of employment in the past five years. Frustration set in as he realized he could contact these former employers, but Ford seemed the type who wouldn't have listed them if he thought they'd give negative responses.

Morrison walked in, a look of determination as he nodded.

"Thanks," Penn said. "I hope you can help me."

He handed the resume to his vineyard manager. "Take a look at the referrals, the past employments Ford listed. He's had three jobs in five years, with no employment in almost a year. He explained it as a number of things. 'Not enough responsibility, not allowed to use his skills, not a good fit with personalities, etc. I let it go for two reasons, One, I needed somebody with his creds, and two, I don't know if that many jobs as a lab worker in five years is normal for this area. And I also don't know any of the people on the list."

Morrison sat. "It's kind of a touchy situation. I didn't say anything before because, as I said, I wanted you to form your own opinions after the interviews. I figured you were sharp enough to pick up Ford's style of nonsense, and you did." He shrugged. "The answer to your question, is no. That kind of moving from job to job is not normal. At least in this wine community."

Almost afraid to ask, Penn nodded. "What about his reasons for job changes?"

"On the face of it, they're true enough. He didn't think any place he worked made the best use of his skills. Because he didn't have a viticulture or enology certificate or degree, he was usually hired to work his way up. But that's not how he saw it."

Penn leaned forward. This was not good news. "Is that last the basis for the personality differences?"

Morrison lightly rubbed his hands together. "Depends on who you talk to. Everyone he's worked for had the same experience. Demands that he knew the process better than them and later, claims that he was the driving force for their best releases."

"I'm assuming there's another side."

"Let's just say Drew works the room. He makes it his business to schmooze all the winery and vineyard owners at every event he attends. A one-man promotional tour. Unfortunately, that's resulted in a number of people who believe he doesn't deserve his questionable reputation at other wineries."

Penn had gotten a hint of Ford's salesman mode during the interview. When asked for his strengths, Drew had talked in great detail. When asked for his weaknesses, he had just shrugged and grinned. "He told me if I hired him, he wanted a contract to protect himself and his contributions to the different successes he would generate."

Morrison raised an eyebrow. "A contract in his favor, no doubt."

"Haven't seen it, but I'll have my attorney vet it." He tapped fingers on his desk. "I wonder what Ford would say if I offered him an 'at will' employment contract?"

"Meaning you'd have the right to terminate him at your discretion."

"Yep. Even if I dislike the color of his socks."

Morrison scratched his neck. "Guess you'd find out how bad he wants to work here."

Penn shook his head and frowned. "With everything else I have going on; I don't need to be pulled into the mix. I'll tell Ford I'm going to continue to look."

Morrison shrugged. "Think you're already in. If he thought his reputation was the reason he didn't get hired, he has enough spite to bring up the rumors surrounding the wineries he's already hurt. Then start spreading rumors about Silver Vines. This business is very competitive. People who took a chance on him are careful about how they respond to his work history with them. If they told the whole truth, their own reputations could get blasted to the point that they might take a long time to recover."

Penn's frown deepened. "Then why did the alliance even give out his name?"

Morrison tapped the resume. "Knowing a couple of them through my wife, I'd say they're staunch members of the Ford fan club."

Shoving his hands through his hair, Penn shrugged. "He'll have to do his worst, then. I'm not taking on that kind of glory hound." He straightened. "Wait a minute. Cady said she'd worked with him. Was that at one of the wineries on his resume?"

The vineyard manager shook his head. "No. At Vines to Water. For half that last year he left blank. You need to ask *her* about it."

"He told me he took classes and worked at his folks' winery in California," Penn said. "Wonder why he didn't just put the St. Simons down as a reference?"

Morrison smiled and bobbled his eyebrows. "Probably because Cady's no fool. She keeps meticulous records of her work, signs them, and stores them digitally. Hard to make claims against that."

Penn couldn't stop his own grin. The more he heard about Cady St. Simon the more he liked. What was it people said about beauty *and* brains? A difficult combination to beat. "That claim being he was the one who developed that amazing cab released last year?"

"Yeah. That one never got much traction because anyone who knows Cady and her parents knows it wasn't true."

Penn stood and held out his hand, his decision to keep the vineyard manager on was reinforced every day. "You've been a big help."

Morrison stood and took the proffered hand. "You have enough going on to keep this place running successfully. Just watch your back where Ford's concerned."

After he left, Penn walked onto his patio and looked toward the St. Simon house. It ticked him off that people like Ford thought nothing of manipulating the truth in their own favor no matter who it hurt.

He turned as Kraken whined and nudged the door open, his gaze pinned across the road. Penn stepped over and grabbed the dog's collar. "It's a good idea boy, but a bit too obvious to appear at her door again and blame it on you. Makes me look lame."

Kraken whined again and tugged.

"You've given me a good idea, though." He walked the beast back inside and closed the door before searching out Siobhan.

"I'm going over to St. Simon's to get a recommendation for a local vet. After Kraken gets groomed, I'll take him in and have him checked over. Also find out the most humane leash since he tends to head over their way every chance he gets."

Siobhan started laughing. "Very creative, since you seem to do the same thing. And the lab being on this side of their property, dropping in on Cady, who also has a dog, would make the most sense."

"You're just mean."

"And you're just transparent."

Busted. There were times he really hated how well Siobhan knew him. He tried to look indignant. "It's a valid reason."

His sister wasn't through. "I saw Rich Morrison leaving. He and JoAnn have a couple of dogs. Why didn't you ask him?"

Penn threw up his hands. "My mind was elsewhere and we had more important things to discuss."

Siobhan's smile faded. "You're serious. What were you talking about?"

"I asked him to help me go over Drew Ford's resume. I had questions that weren't answered during the interview."

She sighed. "Doesn't sound like a good outcome."

"Let's say turning out a prizewinning label's not worth the risk in hiring him."

"Not unhappy he won't be here every day. I *am* unhappy you don't have other options, yet."

Penn rubbed his face. "Let's change the subject. "What smells so good?"

Siobhan grinned and pointed to a single layer cake on a pristine white plate. "Your neighbor brought over a 'welcome to the neighborhood" mandarin orange cake with brown sugar glaze."

"She did? Wow. That is one multi-talented girl."

"Um, if you're talking about Cady, she isn't the only one who lives there."

"Oh. Then her mom brought it?"

Nodding, Siobhan opened a drawer and handed him a cake knife. "The sooner it's gone, the sooner you can take the plate back."

****

Cady frowned at the insistent knocking on her lab door. She unlocked and opened it, shrinking back. It was Drew. "What are you doing here?"

He looked over her shoulder. "How come the door's locked?"

She stood in the doorway, arms crossed. His dark good looks and cognac-colored eyes were certainly appealing, but why had she ever believed he cared for anyone but himself? "New habit I started after your departure."

"Can I come in?"

Cady stayed put. "You haven't answered my question. What are you doing here?"

He held his hands up and grinned. "Truce? Just dropping in on an old partner to let you know I've interviewed at Silver Vines. We're probably going to be seeing more of each other, soon."

It was either an exaggeration or a lie. Drew Ford was practiced in both. On top of which, he wanted something. "Penn hired you?"

"Just a matter of him checking a few details."

Cady cocked her hip and tried to look bored. "Congratulations. Anything else?"

His smile never slipped. "Abbott seems like a thorough guy. In case he talks to my former employers and learns part of the last year I left blank on my resume was spent here, I thought you could throw me a bone for old time's sake. You know, put a shine on our association. It would be a shame if he only heard my side."

And there it was. A favor asked with an implied threat if she didn't comply. "Penn already knows we worked together. He asked for my opinion and I told him I preferred not to comment."

Drew's smile actually reached his eyes. "Good girl. You might pass that on to your parents."

Cady's tolerance died. "You got what you came for. I'm busy." She closed the door and locked it, then listened while his footsteps retreated in the gravel. Well, damn. Three months ago she would've cried or started shaking with anger. Seeing through his thin veneer of charm and closing the door in his face made her day.

She stopped congratulating herself. Drew had seemed pretty confident he'd be hired and working at Silver Vines. Maybe Penn's desperate goal would move him to take a chance. Especially if he overlooked Drew's dicey work history. If she tried to warn Penn, it might look as if she wanted to eliminate him as competition in the Abbott Challenge. She decided to play it by ear. She might learn her brother's hiring plans from Siobhan.

Cady shook her head. She had known the Abbotts for less than a week and couldn't imagine she had any influence. Her thoughts wandered to a future where she did have an influence because she and Penn were more than neighbors. Her stomach flipped. Three days ago she would have said no way. Today, chances tilted toward even. She blinked, surprised her feelings were that strong.

Her phone chirped, breaking her reverie. The screen read Siobhan A. Since her cellphone was on the list of numbers for a tour of Vines to Water, she got an occasional call. "Hello?"

"Hi, it's Siobhan. Do you have a minute?"

Cady held the phone away for a second and re-read the screen frowning. "That's how your name is spelled?"

"Ancient Irish, with an English surname. It's a whole story."

"Good Reader's Digest version, thanks. What's up?"

"I've finished a tentative menu. I hoped you'd have time to match some wines with the items."

"Glad to," Cady said. "Your place or mine?"

"Can we do mine? If I change my mind or decide on another item, I'll want to make sure I have the ingredients."

A ridiculous sense of happiness filled Cady. "Sure, when?"

"How about 6:00, dinner time? I've been working a new chicken and wild rice bake. Would love your opinion. Rich and Penn just gobble up whatever I put in front of them." She made a pffft noise. "Troglodytes."

Cady laughed. "Can I bring anything?"

"Just an appetite. I hid most of the cake your mother brought over so there'd be enough for dessert. Yummy."

"She'll love to hear that. She was a little timid about bringing a homemade cake to a chef."

Siobhan chuckled. "I'm going to ask for the recipe."

"Okay, now you're her new best friend."

More chuckling ensued. "See you at 6:00."

Cady realized she still wore a grin after she hung up. A cheerful invitation from a new friend, or looking forward to seeing that friend's brother again? In both cases, the call had wiped out the bad taste Drew's visit had left.

Chapter Six

Freshly showered, Cady stood in front of her closet, undecided. Why was this a big deal? She knew the answer, but glossed over it. She'd never particularly cared about her wardrobe's limited choices. Short sleeved t-shirts in the summer, long in the winter. Staring for ten minutes didn't change the view. Then she remembered the good stuff.

After the rating on her cab came out, Cady had let Adrienne talk her into a shopping trip to Bellevue Square; mall for upscale shoppers in western Washington. The resulting pieces hung at the farthest side, "being saved for special occasions." The short, flirty, navy dress with big peach-colored flowers had been worn to Adrienne's wedding, but the white Sea Island cotton shirt with stitched-down tucks on the front, and black capris won.

Two hours later, the appreciation in Penn's gaze when he opened the door, confirmed she'd made the right choice.

Penn had also taken some trouble. Although no slouch on the other occasions she'd seen him, he wore bleached jeans and a green, garment-dyed polo shirt.

The green enhancing the flecks in his hazel eyes. On closer examination during dinner, Cady realized classically handsome was a word she wouldn't use for his looks. Penn was more all-American. Blond hair, nice eyes with dark lashes, and a one hundred percent dazzling smile. Like he could be trusted.

She'd brought a bottle of her prized cabernet as a house-warming gift and after a few glasses, told him just that.

Siobhan giggled. "You do know he's a marketing genius. Ice to Inuits and potatoes to Idahoans."

Cady leaned toward Penn and scrutinized his face. "Well *that's* scary. How can you tell if he's sincere?"

"Right here," Penn said. "I'm right here."

Siobhan rolled her gaze up. "Actually, selling aside, he's pretty sincere. And boring. He does have a vulnerable side, though. I'll tell you about it sometime."

"You do that and twin bond or not, I'll have to kill you," Penn said.

"Sorry," Siobhan said, her laughter escalating. "Sorry, sorry, sorry."

Cady's gaze landed on Penn, then Siobhan, then back. "I'm lost."

"Let me," said Penn. "Siobhan caught me cheating at the board game, *Sorry*, when we were kids. I always killed it and she would cry. That made me feel bad, so I *was* cheating, but in order to let her win. To this day, she doesn't believe me. Anyway, the next morning, I found all the game pieces glued to the bottom of my favorite cereal bowl."

I'm falling in love with this man, Cady thought. That doesn't seem possible, but there it is. She hopped up. "Wearing out my welcome. Gotta go."

"Oh," said Siobhan. "Thanks for your help. I'll pick up the wine you paired with the menu and get the invitations out."

Penn stood. "I'll walk you home."

What humiliating thing would she say or do if left alone with Penn? "Really not necessary. I'm good."

His eyebrows drew together. "Then I'll follow you."

She didn't know what to say to that, so gave a finger wave and backed toward the door. True to his word, Penn walked slowly in her direction.

Kraken had been watching from his spot on the floor and stood to leave with them.

Penn grinned. "Guess we're both going."

Cady stopped, noticing for the first time the dog's fur had been dramatically reduced. "Hey, Kraken got a haircut. He looks very . . . um, less monsterish. Like the overgrown puppy he is. It's darling."

"He can't hear you, but don't give out that 'he's such a cute puppy,' look. Or you'll be sorry."

Cady nodded, not looking at the dog, then walked toward her house, aware that Penn and Kraken were shortening the distance behind her. Nearly there, she turned, twilight over her shoulder illuminating Penn, one hand in his pocket, one holding Kraken's new leash.

It wasn't her fault. Some unseen force moved her mouth. "Would you like to see my private beach?"

Penn peered at her. "Um, you have a private beach? How far is it?"

"At the end of our vines."

His gaze made a trip this time, looking past her to the St. Simon vineyard and back. He shrugged. "I'm in."

Sensing there was more to come, Kraken quivered and whined, pulling at the leash.

Penn looked down, grinning. "Guess he's in, too."

Cady turned and walked toward the river, towing her shadow. Penn caught up slowly, Kraken having to stop and sniff at new smells.

Please like it. Please like it, she chanted in her head, then stopped near the edge where the bank dropped to the river. Penn came up behind her and slid his hand down her arm to take her hand. "I like your beach."

That sealed it. Cady turned, looking into eyes that wanted the same thing she did. "I enjoyed the evening."

Penn pulled her close. The kiss was sweet, but once she let the moment settle, sweet wasn't the word for how it played havoc with the rest of her body. "More," she said and pulled his head down for another kiss, hoping it wasn't just a random impulse on his part.

She moved away before complete shame had her dragging him down to the cheatgrass.

"My dog's crazy about you," he said. "Can't be helped." Then he turned and walked back to Silver Vines, his fingers tight on Kraken's leash.

"I am in so much trouble," Cady mumbled.

****

"I think she's onto us, Kraken," Penn mumbled as he towed his straining dog into the kitchen.

"Cady left in a hurry," Siobhan said. "She forgot to take her mom's cake plate. And since you grilled her at length about vets for Kraken, you can always use the plate as an excuse to go over there."

Her grin faded as she studied his face. "Hey. Are you okay?"

"I'm in serious doubt," Penn said. "I just told Cady that Kraken was crazy about her and it couldn't be helped."

His sister tilted her head. "Subtle. Do you think she realized you were talking about you?"

"Probably. Since that was after I kissed her. And she kissed me back."

Siobhan clapped. "I don't care who started it, I *like* it."

"Complicates a lot of things, though. We're in competition, she lives very close, what if it doesn't work out?"

"Oh, for pity sake, talk yourself out of your attraction because it scares you."

Penn considered that. There was some truth to what she said. He wasn't a stranger to kissing pretty women. He *was* a stranger to the other feelings the pretty redhead brought out in him. Feelings that needed naming and sorting. Serious doubt seemed a spot-on description of his situation. "I'll work on it."

Kraken whined beside him. Penn got on his knee and hugged the dog, ruffling his short fur. Kraken took that as an opportunity to pin his master to the floor and wash his face.

****

Penn paced his office, glancing out the window and across the road. It had been two days since Cady came to dinner and he hadn't come to a decision about their close encounter. There was a definite attraction on both sides, but he firmly believed you don't mess your own nest. Or in this case, the one next door. So, he'd decided on cowardice for a while since he couldn't think of anything but Cady and didn't want to run into her until he'd had time to figure out what to do about falling in love at this time in his life.

He saw her drive away and went into his kitchen to retrieve the cake plate. Siobhan stood going through the mail. She looked up and saw him pick up the plate. "Cady not at home?"

Penn sighed. "No. Just left. I'll take this back to her mom."

"Going to have to face it, and Cady. Sometime."

"It, being?"

"That Kraken's not the only one crazy about her. And if you don't do something soon, she's going to think you're just crazy."

He hated it when she was right. "Any suggestions?"

"Let me answer that with a question. Are you still determined to get out a label in time for the anniversary challenge?"

Penn actually had to think about it. The timeline he'd originally thought reasonable to build, furnish, and hire workers for the winery and an enologist for the lab had turned out to be almost double. He lifted a shoulder. "I still want to, but I don't think I can put together the resources to do it on my own."

"And?"

"And I guess I have to go from that reality."

"Then getting positive responses to our party invitations should cheer you up. I got two calls accepting this morning. I'm sure it's a combination of curiosity and welcome but you can also use the opportunity to get referrals for the best equipment and suppliers. Maybe even a spare enologist or two."

Penn smiled. Siobhan was ever the optimist. He tipped his head toward the door. "Going across the road. Be back in a few."

"Coward."

"You bet."

Walking outside he thought for the tenth time how wrong he'd been about the weather here. He thought most of the best climates for growing grapes was in California, but learned different. The southeastern part of Washington was not soggy or rainy like western Washington. And the soil, hot summers and mostly moderate winters was perfect.

Penn tapped on the kitchen door of the St. Simon residence. Surprisingly, Cady's father answered, followed closely by Cady's miniature pinscher, Desi. "Hi, girl." She backed off when he reached for her, then promptly came back and stood on his foot sniffing his jeans.

"Standing on you is a good sign," Cord St. Simon offered. "She probably won't let you pick her up, though."

Penn pulled a doggie bacon treat from his pocket and held it out. Desi backed off again.

Cady's dad laughed. "Cady thinks Desi was royalty in a former life. She'll only take food from her royal staff. Us."

"Um, I brought back your wife's cake plate," Penn said. "It was really great. Tell her my sister would like the recipe."

"Come in. Cady and her mom aren't here right now. In town picking up a few things."

He'd only seen Cady driving. Her mom must have been riding shotgun. "Thank you, sir."

"Call me Cord. How are things going? Are you progressing with your plans for bringing Silver Vines into the winery business?"

Penn nodded. "The expense is huge and will probably take most, if not all of the inheritance I received from my grandfather."

Cord St. Simon smiled. "It's a powerful dream. Helen and I borrowed to the bone. Took us twenty years to get even."

A low whistle escaped Penn. "I count myself lucky."

"Speaking of which," Cord said. "I understand from the Alliance, you're not having much luck finding an enologist. Unfortunately, the wine industry here is growing so fast, the local college can hardly keep up with their viticulture and enology certification and degree enrollments. Too bad that doesn't help you."

"Penn shrugged. "I thought in an area with this many wineries, there would be more than two candidates, at any rate. Since I'm still in the building stage, my next step will be advertising for an enologist. Marketing is my specialty and I mean to use national wine magazines and websites."

"I take it that means you're not going with either of the candidates referred by the Alliance?"

Penn shook his head. "Drew Ford had the qualifications I need, but he didn't seem like a good fit. For one thing, he worked here for a while last year in your lab and omitted it from his resume. I asked Cady for an opinion, but she just said she'd rather not."

Cord nodded. "That covers it."

Penn liked the fact that Cord stood by his daughter's decision not to malign Ford. He could have taken a shot, too, but didn't. It was nice to know his neighbors were down-to-earth people who stood up for each other. His step was lighter on the way home. Great neighbors. He envied their closeness. So, why was he being an idiot about Cady? Did her answer about Drew Ford indicating they had personal differences bother him?

****

Cady helped her mother off-load the groceries into the kitchen. Her dad stocked the pantry at her mother's direction. As Cady passed the kitchen island on her way back to the car, she saw the cake plate on the counter. "When was the plate returned?"

Her dad poked his head around the pantry door. "While you two were gone. I had a nice chat with Penn."

Cady loved her parents, but they both had an illogical need to see her happy. That was part of the problem that developed with Drew. They saw she liked him and encouraged the romance. Or what everyone but Drew saw as a romance. She narrowed her eyes. "Define nice chat."

"He's not going to hire Drew."

Immediate elation filled her. "That's great." Then she had to know the flip side of the coin, "Why not?"

"Said it wasn't a good fit. He found out Drew had worked here this past year and lied about it. That didn't sit well with Penn."

Cady considered her dad's answers. Drew being wrong about working at Silver Vines was the best part, but he would no doubt suspect her as the one who revealed his lie. That was bad. "You know Drew is going to blame us, or me, for not getting hired. And he's vindictive enough to start a new round of rumors."

Her dad nodded. "What do you want to do?"

Good question. Did their kisses a couple of nights ago change her influence with Penn? Maybe influence wasn't the right word. Maybe she just didn't want to tell a man she had new feelings for about what a fool she'd made of herself. Cady sighed. "I'll talk to Penn."

"He's going to put ads in some of the national wine magazines and websites. So, I don't know if he'll tell Drew before he tries all his options, but you might have some time."

Cady's mother stepped out. "We received the invitation for the event at Silver Vines. I accepted. It's mid-week." She shrugged. "Drew might be there. Invited or not."

That was true. Unless an event was for a specific number of people at a sit-down party, Drew thought he'd be welcome anywhere. An attitude Cady used to think was cute and quirky.

She was saved from sharing her introspection with her parents by the ringing of her cellphone. "Hello."

Siobhan's name appeared on the display. "Help."

Cady laughed. Cheered immediately. "What can I do?"

"I told one person who called to accept our invitation. Just one. That I was pairing my menu with local wines and now I've been inundated with offers of bottles. Everyone's so nice. How can I turn them down without hurting feelings or have them thinking we're snobs?"

Cady had dealt with this problem before. "Accept them all and do one of two things. Have lots more parties and use it up, or have the ones you can't use in clever displays. You have plenty of room for that."

"Excellent!" said Siobhan. "Can you come over now and help me decide on some areas for the event? Pleeease?"

Cady realized how much Penn and Siobhan were beginning to mean to her. As an only child, and having put up with Drew's feigned attention, she was ready for this. "Be over in a half hour?"

"Yea! See you then."

Cady's stomach jittered as she ended the call. Going to Silver Vines meant the definite possibility of seeing Penn. Hopefully more thrill than awkward encounter. In which case, she had twenty-eight minutes to shine.

****

Desi trailed her to the door. Intent on taking a walk, too. Sharp barks followed when Cady closed the door and left without her. Glancing back, she almost started to put on Desi's harness and take her along. She shook her head, deciding to put off the doggie meet until she stood on firmer ground with the man who said his dog was crazy about her.

The same man who waited in the middle of the road between their two properties. Smiling.

"Siobhan said you were coming over to help. I thought I'd put myself in your path, and thank you in advance."

Cady was beginning to really like this spot in the road. She grinned. "I haven't done anything, yet."

He took two long strides and pulled her into his arms for a 'knock-your-socks-off' kiss. Guess that answered her question about his first kiss being random, but the physical pull scared her.

Penn linked their fingers. "I'm counting on that to change."

She felt her eyebrows rise. "Then we need to talk."

He pulled her toward Silver Vines. "We'll do a lot of that in between personal stuff. Right now, Siobhan is waiting for us."

Cady tugged back. "Here's the thing. The physical part is way amazing. You're amazing. But a little piece of me is an enologist. I don't jump to conclusions. I measure and test and measure and test again."

Penn stopped and concentrated on her, his head tilted. But he didn't speak, so Cady continued. "I've been down the impulse road and got burned. Not all the other person's fault either. Once bitten, twice shy my grandmother used to say."

A smile grew on his face. "Are you done posting all the safety labels?"

"I . . . didn't realize I was doing that."

"No problem. I totally understand. You also know I'm a marketing guy. I find out what the buyer wants and use it to sell him. In your case, I don't need to sell you to me. It's a no-brainer. You're smart, pretty, a dog lover, and not afraid of life. A rare combination and one I want to be a part of." He grinned. "Plus, you are just flat-out fun to kiss."

Cady let herself be pulled along, no ready response to Penn's last sentence. "I blame you if this craziness comes to a bad end."

Penn laughed, "It won't. The timing sucks, but I'm a realist, and I believe this is real."

Chapter Seven

Siobhan grinned and clapped as they walked into the kitchen, hand-in-hand. "I knew it. He's been moping around and talking to himself for two days. The last time he spent that much energy on a big decision he bought this vineyard and we moved clear across the country. I hate to admit it, but when he's right, he's right."

"Siobhan." A warning note edged Penn's voice.

"I'm still reeling from the impact," Cady said. "And I'm with him so far, but I need to move a teeny bit slower."

Penn gave a curt nod. "Okay. Let's start with this. Will you be my date for our event?"

"That's reasonable," Cady said. "I accept. Now let go of my hand so Siobhan and I can work out the display details."

Penn bent her over for a smacking kiss, then righted her and strutted into the hallway.

Siobhan sniffed. "Arrogant know-it-all."

Cady blinked and turned to her hostess. "Your brother does have a way of letting a person know what he wants and where they stand."

"And if I didn't shoo him away, he'd stand in the way of progress. Uh oh."

Cady turned in the direction of Siobhan's stare and laughed. Kraken was sneaking into the room on his belly, his head low.

"The males in this household are drawn to you like a magnet," Siobhan said, and made a hand sign that had the big dog stand, give a longing look in their direction and leave.

"Our next event isn't for a month," Cady said, willing herself to stay in the conversation instead of following Penn, and Kraken, down the hall. "We have a number of large Plexiglas cubes we can loan you to stack or fill depending on how many extra bottles you're gifted. I think the smoke gray ones will look best in your great room. Since it's warm and you won't have a fire going, they can be situated around the fireplace. What do you think?"

Siobhan nodded. "That sounds good. I'm glad we aren't going rustic, which seems to be the thing nowadays. And which I think looks like a bunch of splinters waiting to snag someone or their clothes."

"How are you fixed for a sound system?" Cady asked. "We have one that's portable and will work with any music subscription. I can bring it over tomorrow in a couple of trips, along with the cubes."

Siobhan rolled her eyes. "Are you serious? I'll lose my good standing as a stellar twin if I don't send Penn over to get those things."

Cady tapped the countertop and lifted a shoulder. "As long as we're speaking of Penn, I hate to poke a good thing, but why hasn't your brother been snapped up, hog-tied, and married?"

"Fair question," Siobhan replied. "He *was* spoken for, in a big way. A girl from a neighboring town who worked summers in our tasting room. The real thing turned out to be not so real when the family imploded after Mom died and Dad remarried."

Cady looked toward the empty hallway. "That's sad. Scares me to think I might be a rebound gap stop for a broken heart."

"Don't lose any sleep. I never saw him get *this* tied in knots around Brittany."

That made Cady smile. "Good to know. Plus, I'm a Scorpio and we are not a forgiving bunch."

"On that note," Siobhan said, sliding her elbows on the counter and cupping her chin, "Mind if I ask what your deal is? That big lunk head of a brother is pretty important to me and I'd hate to see him hurt."

"Fair's fair." Cady said. "Not much to talk about and I'd appreciate it if you didn't share, because it's embarrassing."

Siobhan stood. "Don't mean to pry."

Cady shook her head. "You're not. It involves Drew Ford."

"Oh."

Siobhan was the only other person outside the family and her friend Adrienne she had confided in and Cady hoped it wasn't a wrong step. "He worked with me in our lab last year and I thought there was a definite attraction. Especially when we were alone." She peeked toward the empty hallway. "Turns out, he spread the rumor he'd been 'dropping in' and helping me for a couple of years. Telling people it was him who actually developed the formula for my highly-rated Cab. When I denied he'd helped me, he said it was because I'd had this major crush on him and he wasn't interested."

Siobhan pulled her lips in and wrinkled her nose. "That sucks. He sucks. Growing up with money, I learned early on to see if a boy was interested in me or my father's Dun & Bradstreet rating. Surprising how much it hurts when you learn it's the latter."

Ulterior motives indeed. It hurt enough that there were people Cady had known all her life who believed Drew Ford had developed her cab. She sighed. "Sounds like you're a step ahead of me in that kind of smarts. It took a while, but I decided I contributed to the rumors by not speaking up for myself."

"Just so you know, Penn doesn't play games," the brunette said. "He's so straight forward, it's boring.

And speaking of straight forward, guess I should admit that since this happy couple thing hadn't, um, blossomed this much when the invitations went out, both of Penn's interviewees received one. Both have accepted."

Cady pulled the sides of her mouth down. "Can't hide in the vines forever. And as we're talking full disclosure, I need to tell Penn about a visit I received from Drew yesterday."

"I like this guy less and less," Siobhan said. "What did he want?"

"I'd like to know that, too."

Cady jumped and turned at Penn's voice, trying to keep hers low-key. "Not much. He thought he had the job with you nailed, and asked me not to mess up his chances by telling you about his lie."

Penn pushed away from the doorframe. "I'd already heard about it and decided not to hire him before that. Haven't told him, yet. Now, I'm looking forward to it. Besides, my attorney took a quick look at the ridiculous contract Ford wanted me to sign and said no and hell no."

Cady smiled. Not because of Drew's misfortune and the fact that he wouldn't be working across the road from her, but because the gorgeous man across the room wanted to be with her. "Not that I believe you need the warning, but I learned the hard way, watch your back."

He walked toward her, eyebrows bobbing. "I'd rather watch you."

****

Penn sat at his desk the next morning and considered his new found interest in Cady St. Simon. He stood to pace. No. Interest wasn't a good word. Fascination, crush, infatuation, none seemed strong enough to define his feelings. Which was crazy because he thought he was a level-headed guy. Siobhan said he was falling for their neighbor and nothing he could do but try and stay sane. Then she'd laughed and told him it was fine with her if she added Cady to the family. She left his office still laughing, as he'd said "not helping," to her back.

He rubbed his thumb and forefinger across his forehead, smiling. The thought of marrying Cady had to have been camping in the back of his mind because it didn't scare him as much as he thought it would. She was a different story since she wanted to go slower. This could be the biggest test of his skillset ever. Selling himself to Cady. Slowly. He could do it because he wanted it so badly.

He also still wanted to find an enologist to help him develop his new label. After walking Cady home, Penn spent the afternoon putting ads for enologists online.

Rocking back in his office chair, he let out a long breath. He was now in a wait mode. Waiting for his permits to be approved by the county, waiting to review the final architect plans that incorporated Siobhan's kitchen and dining room, waiting to hear from any interested enologists. He stopped and smiled. Siobhan had told him to give poor Cady a break and wait until afternoon before going over to get the display pieces and sound system for their party. As Cady had also volunteered to help him find a building contractor, that was another reason to spend time with her.

First, the unpleasant business. From what he'd learned of Drew Ford, the guy wouldn't take rejection well. Penn smiled. His attorney had pulled no punches. Advising him that signing Drew's contract would be a big mistake. He pulled out the file holding his interview information, and dialed the number.

"Hey, Boss."

"Um, Drew?"

"The one and only."

"Okay. This is Penn Abbott."

"Been expecting your call."

"I wanted to thank you for your time, but since my lab and winery buildings are still on the drawing board, I'm going to continue to look for an enologist."

"Who've you been talking to?"

"About what?"

"About me."

"I don't understand. You mean the follow up on your references? Yeah, I did that."

Drew's voice flattened. "You know exactly what I mean. The rumor mongers and jealous types out to ruin me."

Penn frowned. The guy was also a little paranoid. "I didn't run into anything like that. My decision was based on widening my options by more than two candidates."

"You're making a big mistake, Abbott."

Ford's attitude of blaming him and or others for not getting the job pissed Penn off. "Again, sorry it's not a good fit. I also told you my attorney would vet your contract. He has, and advised me not to sign. Besides, you have that other offer to consider." Dead air. "Hello?"

"Yeah, see you tomorrow."

Penn was stumped, until he realized Drew was talking about his and Siobhan's party.

"Um, sure. See you."

He hung up and shook his head. Guy could be the best enologist around, but his attitude spelled trouble, and Penn was glad he hadn't hired him.

Dismissing the disagreeable conversation with Drew, Penn scrolled to Cady's number and tapped.

He heard the smile in her voice. "Hello."

He deepened his voice. "Yes, I'm looking for a top-notch beautiful redhead enologist, but I understand you're taken. Can you recommend someone else?"

"Hmmmm, no."

"No, you're not taken, or no, you can't recommend someone else?"

"I mean I'm not the kind of girl that gets taken, and I would be a fool to recommend someone else."

He laughed. "Can't get anything past you. Mind if I come over?"

"Not at all. Got up early and checked the barrels for free sulphurs and put the things we're loaning you on the patio."

Penn felt a prick of pride. Cady St. Simon blew him away. She had hit him hard and fast without trying. And he considered himself a goner and happy about it. "On my way."

Seeing Cady just inside the patio door, Penn swooped in and caught her off guard, turning her in his arms and kissing her, ending her squeal of surprise.

"Um, what's going on?"

Cady sprang away. "Oh. Hi, Dad."

Cord St. Simon frowned. "This is new."

Penn tipped his head. "Yes, sir. Cady is . . . well, it surprised us, too. At least I hope she thinks of this as us."

Cady slipped her fingers between his. "Can't explain it, but I do, Dad."

Penn noticed little improvement in his neighbor's expression.

Chapter Eight

The warmth blooming in Cady's chest from Penn's kiss diminished at the look on her father's face. She glanced at Penn and realized he was puzzled by the cool stare from Cord St. Simon. "Not the same thing, Dad. Not at all."

"How so?" he asked.

Cady turned to Penn. "Drew's employment here ended in professional and personal differences. The professional part, you may have already figured out. He's tried to take credit for good releases at several wineries. Including the cab with the high rating we released. Telling people he 'dropped in,' and helped me during its development. Insinuating the composition was his idea."

"He struck me as the type who makes it up as he goes along," said Penn. "All in his own favor."

"Not only that," said Cord. "He takes advantage of women." He tipped his head toward Cady. "By pretending he has feelings for them. He's basically a user."

"Penn's not like that," Cady said. "He hasn't asked for any favors or tried to talk me into anything."

"Glad to hear it," her dad said, looking from her to Penn and back. "Although it might not have occurred to either of you at this point, but Penn wants to enter the cabernet challenge his father's hosting and he's having trouble hiring a qualified enologist. Cady is one of the best, and she also planned on entering the challenge. That's quite a conflict for two people starting a *personal* relationship."

Penn's fingers tightened on hers. "I understand where you're coming from, sir, and I want you, and Cady, to know that however much the challenge means to me, Cady means more."

Her heart thudded. Penn had just declared his feelings for her in front of her father. Basically, admitting her success was more important than his dream. She smiled and tilted her chin up. "Not the same thing at all, Dad."

This time, Cord St. Simon smiled back. "Then, I hope it works out."

Cady heard a shallow sigh from Penn. She tugged at his hand. "Come on. We have work to do and Siobhan is a stern taskmaster." She grinned. "As am I."

The sigh deepened. "Maybe I should have marketed myself as a strong, silent man-in-command."

She picked up the sound system and handed it to him, taking a couple of display cubes for herself. "Too, late. You've let it slip that you're a full-on mushy guy."

Penn bobbled his eyebrows at her. "I can be anything you want."

"Then, I want you to get moving."

Laughter from her dad followed them out the door and halfway across the road.

The door into the great room at Silver Vines presented a test, as the glass was covered in dog.

"Uh, oh," Penn said. "He must have snuck out of his crate in the office and past Siobhan."

He set down the portable system and leaned to kiss her.

"Hey, not fair," she said. "My hands were full."

"Full hands, cooking, working in your lab, I plan to take advantage whenever the opportunity presents itself."

Kraken bumped against the door, frantic to get at them. Penn made the hand sign Cady recognized as "sit," and the big dog complied, quivering with the attempt.

"I'm going to have to practice that one," she said.

"And see to it that he and Desi get along," Penn replied wryly. "First we'll have to convince him she's not a toy."

Cady laughed. "She'll do that on her own."

Penn walked to the door and presented another sign. Kraken left, casting a yearning glance as he walked away.

"Busted," said Penn. "We'll need to make sure the door to the office is closed for the next couple of days while we get ready. Otherwise, we won't get anything done." He peered through the glass. "All clear."

They positioned the pieces they'd carried over and Penn went back for the rest of the display cubes while Cady set up the sound system, hooking it up to an ad-free music subscriber. Siobhan came in as she was finishing. "That sounds nice. We have almost one-hundred percent acceptance from the invitees. Now, I'm getting nervous. I'm used to overseeing the kitchen for these events, not playing hostess."

"Are you kidding?" Cady asked. "The whole wine community will think the two of you are adorable. And be prepared for everyone asking you for your recipes."

Siobhan smiled. "That I can do. Most of them are pretty simple."

Penn walked in carrying more display cubes. "Who's pretty simple?"

"You, lunk head," Siobhan quipped, then turned to Cady. "I'm counting on your help. Point out people and remind me of names and their weakness for food and kinds of wine. Who donated what wine, that kind of stuff."

"Wait a minute," Penn said. "You can't just draft my date as your spy."

"Oh, man up," Siobhan said. "You guys are going to have lots of time to spend with each other." She clapped and executed a cute shimmy. "And I might be getting a sister. Yea!" With that, she turned and went back to her kitchen.

Penn made a dismissive noise after her, then looked around before pulling Cady to him for a kiss.

She pulled away, reluctantly. "What did she mean by that?"

"Don't pay any attention to her. She's been talking as if you're already part of the family. Wishful thinking."

"Scary thinking," she corrected with a mock shudder.

He pulled her back into the hug. "I remember what you said about slower, and I promise I'm taking it to heart."

Cady tipped her head back. "We don't even know each other's middle names."

"Not important," Penn said, avoiding her gaze.

She laughed. "That bad?"

He sighed and his shoulders slumped. "Family thing. Siobhan got the worst of it, but I came in second. Middle name's Forsythe. Please don't tell me it's a deal breaker."

She gave him a quick peck on the cheek. "Take more than that. Mine's Leigh. And I'm here to help Siobhan, so the rest of our fun will have to wait until your party."

****

Cady was late. She'd intended to run her labs, help Siobhan, then take an hour to shop for a new dress. She huffed a long breath. Her mind had been on Penn and she'd dropped two test tubes with contents that had been tested, but not recorded, and she'd had to start over.

She'd gone over to Silver Vines earlier, in hopes of seeing Penn for a few minutes, but he was with Morrison in the vines. Siobhan had the house decorated, but an ingredient crisis had developed in the kitchen. Cady offered to drive into town and pick some up which then left no time to shop for a dress. Poor planning.

Now, she stood in a towel and strappy tan sandals and stared at her closet again, hands on hips. Drew Ford could take a flying leap. She was going to wear the navy-blue dress with peach-colored flowers. It looked good on her and she wanted to impress Penn. Doubt slipped in as she put it on. Penn Abbott was an amazing man who came from a totally different social level, wine royalty. What did he see in her?

Cady shrugged. Her family was well respected and had solid roots in this community. Drew Ford had betrayed and had them believing he wanted to be part of their world. She smiled. That was done and hurt less every day. Now, Penn would stand with her, and that made all the difference.

She walked into the kitchen and her parents turned. "You look nice. Ready?" her mom asked.

"Thanks." Cady responded. "You guys clean up good, too."

Desi trotted to the door and sat. Confident that she was included in the invitation. "Nope," Cady said. "Not this time, girl. The two of us will go over and introduce you to Kraken tomorrow." Desi barked her disapproval and had to be shooed from the door.

They arrived at Silver Vines and were greeted first by Siobhan, then a couple the St. Simons had known for years. The wife whispered, "Aren't the Abbotts sweet? I hear she's a fantastic cook and he wants to start his own label. It's good getting new blood here."

Cady smiled. "I agree."

Penn walked in and came straight over. Every molecule in Cady's body did the happy dance and she almost laughed out loud. He wore tan chinos and a navy-blue polo shirt with pink trim inside the collar. He took her hand. "You look great."

Cady cut a glance at her parents' friends. The wife whispering to her husband. Oh, well. They'd find out soon enough she and Penn cared for each other. "Thank you. Maybe next time I'll call and let you know what I plan to wear."

Penn frowned and stepped back, taking in her outfit without letting go of her hand. Then the similarities hit him and his smile widened. "I only saw you."

He might as well have handed her a slice of the moon. It was the nicest thing anyone had ever said to her and she could see he meant it.

Too flustered to say anything, Cady steered him to the couple. "Have you met the Martins? They're members of several wine clubs and Mr. Martin is the contractor I told you about, Penn. Maybe the two of you could get together."

Penn shook hands. 'I'd be very interested in your views of area contractors and their availability, sir."

"Absolutely, Penn. Cady can get you my number. Give me a call." Then he winked and moved his gaze to Cady. "I see you're fitting into the neighborhood."

"Yes, sir. I like the neighborhood just fine."

She and Penn made the rounds for the next fifteen minutes and were joined by Siobhan. "Everyone is raving about your food," Cady said.

Siobhan nodded. "You were right. I've been asked for several recipes, so I put a pad and pencil by each dish and have promised to email those who want that recipe."

"You clever thing," Cady said. "Brownie points headed your way." She tipped her head at Mason Pritchard. "I also think you have an admirer."

Siobhan sighed. "If I was fishin', I'd have to throw him back. Not mature enough. He did volunteer to do dishes, though. He's on the right track for some girl."

Cady's laugh died when Drew Ford walked in, his gaze focused on her and Penn. Then he pretended to ignore them and work the room, walking up to people with a smile. A few accepted his overtures, but most had strained looks when he approached. He avoided the St. Simons.

"I got this," Siobhan said. "No one's allowed to ruin my first party at Silver Vines." She put on a brilliant smile, walked over, and tugged Drew toward the kitchen.

Penn slipped Cady's hand in the crook of his arm. "Let's go to my office and take a break."

"I'm okay," she said. "He's nothing more than an annoyance."

"I want you to be more than okay," Penn responded. "Besides, I can sneak in a few kisses there."

Cady felt her shoulders relax. "I like the sound of that."

They went down the short hallway into his office. Penn pulled her to him and kissed her thoroughly. "Been looking forward to this all day."

"Me, too," Cady said. "I came over earlier to get a Penn fix but you were working in the vines."

"Remind me to buy a bullhorn," he said. "We'll come up with a code you can use to get me back to the house, so I don't miss anything."

She loved his sense of humor. Penn Abbott was the whole package. "A little drastic, but I wouldn't argue with the results."

"Looking pretty cozy, you two."

Cady jumped at Drew's voice, but Penn just frowned. "This is private, Ford. None of your business. Go on back to the party."

Drew wore a malicious grin. "This is way more fun. You're a fast worker, Abbott. It took me a month to get her to shed that modest little lab apron she wears."

Penn squeezed Cady's hand and took a half-step toward the other man. "You're a real piece of work."

"I've heard the sad little story about why you're here," Drew responded. "If that's the way you want to play the game, I'll be glad to spread it around."

Cady bit the inside of her lip. She wanted badly to slap Drew's face.

"I don't play games," Penn said. "Here's the story I'll be circulating, starting today. 'Contrary to what you've heard, I'm here to establish a west coast location for Abbott Estates Wines. My father wants to expand and sent me to set up the winery and hire only the best.' If anyone asks, I didn't hire you because you're not only not qualified, you're a liar."

"I have way more contacts than you," Drew spat. "So, who are people going to believe?"

"Penn's word will be backed up by the St. Simons," Cady put in. "And we've been here a lot longer than you. Plus, he's a marketing genius. Capable of selling anything."

"Imagine yourself wandering among the dozens of wineries around Lake Okanogan in Canada, or through the Willamette Valley wineries in Oregon. No one will hire you because an Abbott has put out the word." Penn nodded. "I can do that."

Drew straightened. "I might just hang around the area long enough to see your little love match implode. You both want to be recognized in the Abbott Challenge. She could use your grapes and you could use her enology expertise." He gave a nasty laugh. "Who will win and who will walk?"

It came to Cady in a flash and she grinned. "You're misinformed. Penn and I are putting out a label together. We're thinking of calling it Silver Vines to Water. Catchy name, don't you think?"

A muscle worked in Drew's jaw.

Penn was silent.

Cady thought she'd made a huge mistake when he let go of her fingers and walked to the office door that led to the patio. "You heard it straight from the lady. Now, get out."

Penn closed the door after Drew left, but Cady didn't let go of a breath until he turned and came to her in four long strides.

He picked her up and swung her around. "*You are amazing.* That was a stroke of genius. Ford won't know you made it up because he'll be long gone."

Cady showered his face with kisses. "I didn't."

Penn set her down, with a puzzled expression. "What?"

She closed her eyes, hoping with all her heart she was making the right decision. "I didn't make it up. It's what I want. For us. If you're with me."

"I won't let you compromise your chances," he started.

She smiled. "Thinking you can control what I want is your first mistake, Abbott. I want it because we're a team, and I'm falling in love with you. Abbott and St. Simon would be unbeatable."

"Not as unbeatable as Abbott and Abbott," he said, because I'm falling in love with you, too."

Epilogue

Three months later, Penn and Cady stood under a white canopy on their beach and kissed. Wedding guests clapped and Helen St. Simon dabbed her eyes.

Tables covered in navy-blue cloths spread out on either side, with centerpieces of peach and cream peonies circling wine bottles. The bottles were empty, but displayed labels dated a vintage yet-to-come of a Silver Vines to Water cabernet. Each guest would be gifted a bottle when the wine was released.

The bride's new sister-in-law toasted the happy couple and wished them bon voyage on their honeymoon tour of the Bordeaux region in France.

A big, goofy, dog of undetermined origins and a miniature pinscher each wearing a bow of white organza, circled the guest's tables, hoping for droppage.

Made in the USA
Coppell, TX
29 July 2020

31913894R10167